Praise for
Where You Come From Is Gone

"Christopher Johnston has written an unforgettable novel about family bonds, the pleasure and pain of hard work, and the forces at work against rural communities. In prose that's as laconic as the fishermen, mink farmers, and politicians that fill this novel, the story of this family comes blistering to life. What an homage to a way of life and to the northern Minnesota temperament. What a tremendous reminder of how long the struggle's been real. And what a testament to excellent storytelling."

—Peter Geye, author of *The Ski Jumpers* and other novels

"*Where You Come From Is Gone* is a haunting tribute to fathers and sons, brothers and uncles, wives and mothers, and the family business that sustains them, until it no longer can. In commanding prose that is equally at home on land or over water—in the stink of a mink ranch, along smoke-swept prairies, on the swells of a fishing boat—Christopher Johnston deftly navigates leaving home and coming back in a story of heartbreak spanning three generations whose people are caught between the life they want and the life they get."

—Carol Dunbar, award-winning author of *The Net Beneath Us*

"*Where You Come From Is Gone* is a raw and moving story of a way of life lost to history. The novel follows one generation of a family in the small northern Minnesota town of Worland, where they operate commercial fishing and mink farming businesses. The details are vividly rendered by author Christopher Johnston, who clearly has done his research if not lived it. The story is both engaging and tragic. Most highly recommended.

—Kurt Johnson, Minnesota Book Award winner for *The Barrens*

"*Where You Come From Is Gone* weaves a complex choreography of private longings, solitude, and faults driven by the struggles of a Midwest family to keep their businesses and their bond afloat. Edgy and moving, this novel reflects on the complexity of the search for connection and meaning in life. It poses questions on identity, legacy, and adaptation to change we are all driven to ask ourselves. Christopher Johnston creates an emotional journey with powerful characters who take the reader with them and won't let go even after the book is closed."

—Rosanna Staffa, author of *The War Ends At Four*

"In this stunning debut novel, Christopher Johnston brings to life a border town on Lake of the Woods. *Where You Come From Is Gone* follows half a century of the Brennan family, whose identity is forged in the twin vocations of commercial fishing and raising mink. In vivid and unsentimental prose, Johnston evokes the smell, sound, and texture of net fishing on an inland sea and of harvesting mink. Johnston understands as few authors not only class and the rural/urban divide, but also the nature of work and the bittersweet love of place. The book gutted me on many levels. *Where You Come From Is Gone* is a bracing addition to the literature of the Minnesota-Canadian borderlands."

—Carla Hagen, award-winning author of
Hand Me Down My Walking Cane and *Muskeg*

WHERE YOU COME FROM IS GONE

CALUMET EDITIONS

Minneapolis

10 9 8 7 6 5 4 3 2 1
ISBN: 978-1-962834-35-3

Cover and book design by Gary Lindberg

WHERE YOU COME FROM IS GONE

CHRISTOPHER JOHNSTON

CALUMET
EDITIONS
Minneapolis

For the people who lived it.

"Where you come from is gone, where you thought
you were going to never was there, and where you are
is no good unless you can get away from it."

—Flannery O'Connor, *Wise Blood*

Part I: Pete

One: August 1960

On the day after I got home from the service, I rejoined the crew of my father's fishing boat. Dad put me at the helm for the forty-five-minute trip from Worland to our nets off Buffalo Point. The bison-head-shaped peninsula juts out from Canada into Lake of the Woods. It was the last day I stood on my own.

In the cold water off the point, schools of tullibees roam near the sandy bottom. Walleye and sturgeon grow fat feeding on the spring and fall tullibee runs. For sixty-five years my father and grandfather had set pound nets to catch them. It irritated my family that our town was named Worland. My grandfather started the lake's first commercial fishing operation long before Calvin Worland began turning logs into lumber.

As we entered Muskeg Bay from the Worland River that morning, Swede Carlsen took off in his float plane to haul mail and sportsmen to the Northwest Angle. Dad and the crew, Jim Thunder and Moose Johnson, waved their hats. They pointed at me in the pilothouse. I leaned out the door. The plane's shadow passed over the sparkling water. Swede tipped the wings.

A stiff northwesterly pushed five-foot whitecaps and the boat heaved as we approached the first net. The boat and I were twenty-one years old at the time. Dad built the thirty-foot craft out of Florida cypress, launching it in the spring of 1939. He'd bent the hull planks in a fixture he designed to form precise curvature. Her gray hull was rough and pitted from the epoxy paint he'd used. It reminded me of the moon's surface. The maroon pilothouse was decorated with a gold M above the front window. For me, it symbolized Dad's engineering degree and his expectations— expectations I'd already failed to meet.

I lined up the boat with the pound, the section of the net that holds the fish. Moose, six foot four inches tall and my father's right hand man, held the stern line. He'd seen every mistake I'd made on the boat. Jim Thunder, the local Ojibwe chief, worked next to Moose organizing fish boxes. Dad stood in the bow, back stiff, holding onto the starboard gunwale with his left hand, his right hand raised palm out.

I cut power so Dad could loosen the pound lines as the boat glided past.

"Pete! Too goddamn quick! Don't you remember how to do anything?"

That was the old man's method: tell you what you did wrong, stinging you with a small insult to make sure you didn't forget. The one thing I didn't forget was that I wasn't very smart. Unlike my brothers Lance and Wayne or my sister Mary, explanations didn't stick for me. I learned by doing. Dad understood. He told me before I left for the Army that experience and hard work can make up for a lack of talent.

During my time in the Army, I loathed taking orders. The dusty European cathedrals, museums, and universities bored me. I loved the lake's open solitude in summer and its frozen expanse in winter. It was my fifteen-hundred-square-mile playground. Every day in the Army I thought of getting back on the water. I wanted Dad's life on the lake. The life he had not wanted for himself.

I brought us about and allowed the boat to drift in between the pound and lead pilings. Dad and Moose secured the mooring lines. With the helm tied in place, I went out on deck.

"I need to take a leak before we get started."

Dad turned in the bow. "Good idea. If the game warden or some sportos come along, they'll get the right greeting."

We lined up on the port side, arranged tallest to shortest like a family photo. Moose at the stern, then Jim, me and Dad.

"You sure we're pointing downwind?" Jim said.

"You're the Navy man." Moose laughed. "You should be telling us."

The boat rolled over the waves, making it difficult to stand in place. Our urine streams hit the water at a constantly changing height. We zipped up and Moose turned to me.

"This reminds me of when Mary came out last year."

"What happened?" I pulled up my oiler braces.

"She wanted to do a painting of us working, so she came out to do some sketches. One day we were at this very spot, and she says she has to go."

"I looked for the bailing bucket and realized I'd left it on the dock after washing the deck." Dad closed the snaps of his oiler jacket. "I didn't know what to do."

"Your dad and me each took an arm and a leg. We lifted her up to get her rear end over the side. Good thing she's small."

"She threw the bucket at me after we got in." Dad pointed above his right eye. "Gave me four stitches and this scar." They both chuckled.

Jim asked if I liked the Army. I told him I hated the useless marching and rigid discipline. The only fun I'd had was pulling a couple shifts of guard duty with Elvis while our outfits were on maneuvers.

We hauled a section of net over the gunwale. Jim held up a fish. "Brothers, thank you for your lives, for helping us grow strong, and may you rise again." He tossed the fish overboard.

"Any news from St. Paul?" I asked.

"You wouldn't believe what those bastards pulled in the last session. They've allowed *experimental* gear," Dad replied.

"Why? Who's behind it?"

"The new state Game and Fish Director. He wants to set up a commercial fishing monopoly for his friends."

"And what, exactly, is experimental gear?"

"Trawlers."

We reached over the side to haul again. "You mean like ocean trawlers? With a giant net that snares everything from the bottom up?"

"That's right. No northerns, perch, or muskie for the anglers. No walleye, sturgeon, or tullibees for us. I went to the Capitol to fight it, and you know what the vindictive prick does? He threatens to have a pound net ban added to the bill."

"The state always wants a cut of the action." Jim looked out over the water. "My people fished from the Northwest Angle for a thousand years. They took away gill netting without batting an eye. Now they're going to kill the lake. Even the sportos from the Cities will hate that."

"I hope they do."

"Dad, you really think they'd help us?"

"I'm betting the mink farm on it."

"We could buy mink feed instead of catching it."

"No, the shipping expense would kill us. A fish diet is low cost and produces lustrous fur. I figured that out thirty-five years ago when I started the mink farm. It's why we're still in business today."

We took up positions to bail the pound with a power dipper. I operated the controls while Jim and Moose handled the dipper.

"Ready?" I said.

Moose nodded. Jim lowered the dipper into the pound and gave the thumbs up. I engaged the power take-off and the dipper rose out of the pound full of fish. Jim held the handle steady, and Moose guided the frame. Dad pulled the slipknot at the bottom of the dipper, releasing the fish into four wood boxes. Stray fish flopped onto the deck.

I doubted sportsmen from the Cities would support us. For decades, they'd tried to close Lake of the Woods to commercial fishing. They initiated the Northwest Angle gill net prohibition. The outdoor columnists for the Twin Cities newspapers took every opportunity to describe how we were destroying the game fish population. On top of that, resort owners and their politician-angler friends controlled the natural resources committees in the legislature.

"Pete! Wake up! You've let the take-off cable go slack. It's come off the pulleys." Dad glared at me. "Get your head out of your ass."

The dipper floated in the pound with a tangle of cable piled on the handle. My heart hammered and my shoulders tightened. I thought I'd shed those adolescent feelings of failure in the Army. Instead, disappointing my father still brought a stab of shame. Moose pulled the slack cable on board. I rethreaded the cable through the winch pulleys on top of the pilothouse. On deck, I re-attached the cable to the power take-off.

"Ready?"

Moose nodded. Jim lowered the dipper into the pound and gave the thumbs up. I engaged the power take-off and that was it. The cable looped up to my left knee, tightened and sawed through my leg. Searing pain spread upward from my knee. I collapsed backward onto the fish-covered deck. A bloody loop of cable flew up. Jim appeared from around the fish boxes.

"Arthur, hold him down!"

After that, I remember fragments. Rolling over facedown into the thrashing fish on the deck. Jim and Dad yelling. My belt snapping when it got pulled from my pants. Moose's eyes, wide and glazed. A frightening tension in my forehead. The buzz of Swede's airplane.

"I'm. going. to. pass. out." It took full concentration to say each word.

"Bullshit!" Jim's face hovered over mine. "Stay with me. You're doing great. I heard guys in the Pacific make more noise over less." His voice started to sound slow and stretched. "Just… look… at… my… face…"

"I. need. a. drink." My teeth slammed together.

Jim pried open my mouth and Dad splashed in whiskey from his flask.

"*Sláinte*, son. You're going to make it, goddamnit!"

A warm sensation spread from my throat to my chest. The boat's engine roared to life. Jim tightened my belt around my thigh. Cold spray came over the gunwale, and the wind blew it dry on my face. Hundreds of dying fish writhed against my arms, twisting as they gasped for life. I became one of them, twisting, nearly dead, hoping to be swept over the side to water and salvation.

Jim slapped the side of my face. "Pete, drink this."

He pushed my jaw apart with his fingers. Lukewarm coffee dribbled down my throat. The engine whine shifted lower. *Almost there. Almost there.* I spotted the Buffalo Point dock pilings.

Jim hooked his arms under my shoulders. "Moose, get your arms under his behind."

They lifted me onto the dock. Another bolt of pain shot from my knee up into my thigh. Overhead I saw the blue and yellow wing of Swede's plane rocking with the waves. Two middle-aged men looked down at me through the plane's side windows. A perfect outdoor catalog photo.

Swede strapped me down in the back next to the mail bag, a float cushion under my head. The plane rose, twisted and dropped, over and over again. Radio chatter and Swede's voice blended with the drone of the engine. I desperately wanted some water. I tried to count backward to stay conscious, only to find I'd drifted off each time my head bounced on the cushion and jolted me awake.

They rolled me through the emergency entrance at the back of Worland Hospital. A green-eyed nurse leaned over the gurney.

"You're going to be okay. We'll take care of you."

The gurney slammed through the emergency room doors, and I blacked out.

Two: August 1960

Wayne strode into my hospital room the next morning with a big smile. It had been four years since I'd seen him— his two years in the Air Force followed by my two years in the Army. The little I'd heard about him came in Mom's letters. He'd become a stranger, but as soon as I saw him I recognized my wild, athletic older brother.

He grabbed the bed rail and shook it. My body vibrated from the pain. He laughed. Wrinkles had formed around his eyes and mouth since I last saw him. His auburn hair stuck out the sides of his cap and drooped over his ears. A red welt protruded from the left side of his forehead. He looked nothing like the crew cut hockey player I admired growing up. He grabbed my right hand and shook it, sending more pain rattling down my leg.

"Saint Peter! I'll be damned! You're finally home. I'd ask how you are, but I betcha feel like shit."

"I do." I hated it when he called me Saint Peter, and he knew it. If I showed any irritation, he'd do it more. His greatest joy after hockey and drinking was picking on people.

"Well don't worry. There's a cute nurse out there who looks intent on making you feel a whole lot better."

"No woman is going to be interested in a one-legged fisherman."

"You never know. Captain Ahab had a wife."

"You smell like shit. Dad got you working at the mink farm?"

"You're damn right he does. I've been busting my ass since the day I got back from the service."

"He started on me before we got to the first net."

"I'm not surprised. So, what the hell happened out there?"

"Dad didn't tell you?"

"He didn't say much. Only that you'd managed to take your own damn leg off."

"I don't want to talk about it." I didn't need Wayne piling on about what a stupid mistake I'd made.

He pulled a chair from the corner of the room up next to the bed. "God, you were a sophomore in high school the last time I saw you."

"Forget high school. How was Alaska? I can't believe you're married and running the mink farm. You have a kid now! What the hell happened to you?"

Wayne launched into his story without hesitation. I knew once I got him started on Dad and the mink farm, he'd be hard to stop. They'd surely butted heads over how to run the place and it would keep Wayne's attention on his favorite subject—himself—and away from me.

He began with the day he got back from Alaska, a late April afternoon in 1958. Mom and Dad met him at the Northern Pacific depot. It was warm with a clear sky. Strange for that time of year. Inside the train it was hot from the sunlight pouring in through the windows. He left his window shade up so he could see the countryside. Instead of his uniform, he wore dungarees and a plaid shirt. He'd rolled up his sleeves and undone the two top buttons of his shirt. After two years on an Alaskan Air Force base, he didn't care what the other passengers thought, in their suits and ties and dresses. It felt great to be comfortable.

When he walked down the aisle to get off the train, the passengers looked relieved that he hadn't tried to rob or kill them. Mom and Dad stood on the platform, Mom in her white nursing uniform and Dad in his fishing clothes; a khaki shirt and oil-stained work boots. Dad gave him a tight smile and extended his arm. Wayne said Dad's hand felt cold and mottled, like damp tree bark.

"Welcome home, son."

Mom hugged him.

"Welcome home. It's so good to see you."

"I thought I would never get out of there. The days were endless. Either all sun or all darkness. A couple guys from Alabama lost their minds and refused to leave their bunks. The MP's had to drag them out of the barracks."

Mom looked away with watery eyes. "Are you okay? Did something happen to you up there?"

"Nothing happened. I loaded airplanes."

Dad put his hands on Wayne's shoulders.

"Wayne, you know better than to dress like this for the train. Your shirt is open, your sleeves bunched up."

"Dad, I've been wire tight for two years in the middle of nowhere. I wanted a comfortable trip home."

Mom leaned forward and spoke into his ear. "Wayne, it's not the shirt. It's those tattoos." She looked at him the same way the passengers had on the train. He tried to give her his best charmer smile.

"Mom—"

"We can talk about it when we get home." Dad put his arm around her shoulder.

"Mom, I spent the last year loading H-bombs onto B-36s, never knowing if the world was about to be incinerated." Wayne told me the conversation reminded him of trying to explain away the musky smell of his clothes after a night smoking in the woods with his friends.

The station agent approached with Wayne's duffel. "Welcome home." Wayne thanked him and slung the blue bag over his shoulder.

"Where's Pete?"

The rail car couplings banged together from the pull of the locomotive. The train rumbled onto the Worland River trestle. "He left a week ago for induction into the Army," Dad replied.

"How did he handle it?" Wayne figured the Army would break me. The last time he'd seen me, I was a sixteen-year-old kid who kept to himself.

"He's tougher than you think." Dad stared at the tattoos on Wayne's arms and neck. "He's on his way to becoming a real lake man. Might handle the service better than you did."

"We'll see about that." Wayne turned to Mom. "So, you wrote me that there's some big news about Lance? I already know he's nearly finished his PhD."

Mom's eyes brightened. "He proposed to that girl at Smith College. The wedding is this August in Boston. Has to have everything her way. She's a real piece of work."

Dad smiled at Mom, mischief in his eyes. "Ginny, you'd probably like her a whole lot more if you weren't so similar. Her name is Guinevere Linnehan. Black hair and blue eyes. A real stunner. She goes by Gwen, and she's smart, like your mother."

"When did you meet her? Did Lance come home while I was away?"

"No, we went up to Boston after the fur buyers show in New York."

"What else do you know about her?"

"She's an only child. Grew up east of the Cities on a dairy farm in Wisconsin. They didn't have plumbing and electricity until after the war. Her father put her in a Catholic boarding school after her mother died." Dad shrugged. "I like her. She has fire."

Mom put her hand on Dad's shoulder. "And, she said she wasn't going to get married in some farmville in the Midwest. It had to be Boston. Graduation and marriage in one fell swoop. It's terrible how she pushes him around. It's too much too soon."

"It's not like *we* waited around to get started." Dad took Mom's hand and kissed it. "I'm sure you'll set her straight whenever they do manage to get here."

Wayne leaned on his upright duffel. He pulled a roll-your-own from his breast pocket. He lit the cigarette and snapped his lighter a few times. He couldn't stop the scowl on his face. Lance with his stunning wife and a PhD in plant genetics, while he was back in Worland, an athletic failure and college washout. He wished he had a beer to go with the smoke.

"How's Mary?"

They looked at each other, clearly deciding who should speak. After a moment, Mom replied. "She's fine. She stayed after school to paint. I think she's going to prom with Eddie Worland. I've tried to discourage it, but that probably makes it worse."

Dad curled his arm around Mom's waist and squeezed her. "Eddie's not a bad kid. I'm sure they'll have a little summer romance and then go their separate ways. They're too different. Eddie is like Cal. You can almost see the gears turning in his mind. And Mary, she doesn't plan anything."

"Ah, the artiste moved by inspiration." Mary had been a girl when he left. It was hard to imagine her in high school, going on dates and having big plans. He hauled the duffel onto his shoulder, like a bag of failures he would carry the rest of his life. He took a drag on his cigarette and blew a smoke ring. "Let's go home." The ring sagged and collapsed in the light breeze.

"Don't worry." Dad rattled the keys and change in his pockets. "I've got plans for you."

The next morning, Dad and Wayne drove out to the mink farm, which sat on twenty acres ten minutes west of town. While he was away, the state had installed a stop light at the T where Lake Street met State Highway 11. Wayne looked at the empty road while the turn signal clicked.

"Mom didn't have much to say after we got home."

"She had plenty to say to me after you went to bed. Boy, does she hate those tattoos. You know, it took everything she had not to cry at the station."

"Dad, everyone in the service gets them."

The light turned green.

"Look, I don't want to argue. I need your help, at least while Pete is in the service." His fingers gripped at the wheel as if he couldn't find a comfortable way to hold it. "Can you do that?"

"I don't know what I want to do. I've been home less than a day."

They turned west off the highway onto the gravel road to the ranch. Stones popped and banged against the undercarriage. Brown fields extended to the horizon on either side of the road. The two-story ranch building appeared in the distance. It had been raw framing when Wayne left. Now it was complete. Black letters nailed into the white siding spelled it out:

A. J. Brennan and Sons'
Mink Farm

Wayne chuckled over how the lettering indicated multiple sons owned the business. In fact, Lance, Wayne and I owned nothing. The lettering also made clear Mary's position in the family business.

The ranch building sat at the end of the road. About a quarter mile past the building, the Worland River veered sharply south, then east, then south again. It formed a moat around the property. The mink sheds resembled Quonset huts. A post and steel-mesh fence with an electric wire along the top surrounded the sheds.

Dad parked in front of the two garage doors. The still-frozen river snapped and groaned in the warming weather. He looked around the yard, then turned to stare at Wayne—hard.

"If you're going to run this place, you need to handle yourself better when things don't go your way."

"Dad—"

"I get it. The service is hard. Guys drink, they get tattoos. They want a souvenir of their travels. Jim has an anchor and a hula girl."

"Dad—"

"No." He pointed his index finger at Wayne's nose. "You have *Cut Here* on your throat and a dotted line around your neck. Isn't it bad enough that the world could be blown up at any minute? Do you need to remind everyone of it with a mushroom cloud on one arm and a Jolly Roger on the other?"

"Dad—"

"You're a smart, capable young man. You got a hockey scholarship and finished most of an engineering degree, but you look like you're fresh out of prison, not honorably discharged from the service."

"Dad, I could've made the NHL, but that UND guy slashed me. I missed the rest of the season. You were there. Blood and teeth all over the ice. You saw it."

"Yeah, I did, and it broke my heart. I also thought you would overcome it."

"Dad, I couldn't concentrate. My head hurt all the time. I still have trouble keeping my balance."

"Look, you knew as soon as you dropped out you'd get a draft notice. I feel bad about what happened. We all have to deal with fate and failure. I finished at the U during the Depression. I couldn't get a job. It destroyed my dreams. I came home determined to start over, and built two businesses. You can succeed too—if you're willing to help run this place."

They started with feeding. The feed cart was parked under a tin awning off the backside of the building. Next to the awning was a large stainless-steel tank that stored mink feed—ground fish and bone meal. The feed cart looked like a red Zamboni, one of those ice-resurfacing machines used between periods at a hockey game, except it was driven from the front like a car. Dad had welded the frame and feed tank himself, while the engine and gearbox came from a riding mower.

"You remember how to load and drive it?"

"Yes." Wayne removed the cap from the tank on the feed cart. He lined up the filling hose with the port on the tank. "I never thought I'd have to do this again." The feed made a hissing sound as it flowed through the hose.

"Listen, the fur market is booming. If we do this right, we can make a lot of money for ourselves. We could make the Worlands look poor. Is it a comfortable job in a clean office? Hell no, but since when did you like taking orders from anyone or spending the day indoors?"

When the feed cart was full, Wayne hung the hose on the hook next to the storage tank. Dad pushed his cap back on his head.

"The week since Pete left has been pretty rough on your mother and me. I haven't told her, but I think I'm getting a hernia, and she's been working long hours at the hospital. They're short staffed. The fur market is good, but the state is threatening the fishing business. If we lose that, we lose everything. Now I know you can run this place properly. If you do, I'll give you a stake."

"Dad, I can work on the lake if lifting hurts. The work here's easier."

"No. You never liked working with Moose and Jim. The work here is solitary, which I think suits you. It'll give you time to figure out if this is what you really want. If you need help, Jim and I can lend a hand. After all, Jim got me started in this business. If it doesn't work out, you can at least save some money and go back to college."

Dad must have thought about it for months, probably while putting up that lettering. He was always waiting around the next corner, as if he knew what we were going to do before we did.

And that was it. Wayne climbed onto the feed cart and drove to the west end of the property. To feed the mink, he drove down the center aisle of each shed, stopping at each cage to squirt some feed onto the top. The feed was thick enough to cling to the mesh, so the animals could get on their hind legs and stretch upward to eat. Dad walked to the opposite end of all sixty-two sheds and watched Wayne drive toward him. If he lingered too long or applied too little food to the top of a cage, Dad's voice would boom through the shed. "Too goddamn much!" or "Get going. We haven't got all day!"

Feeding took three hours. In the last hour, damp snow fell, turning the ground into a mash of grass, mink shit and mud. A couple times, the cart lost traction and slid into a shed post. After Wayne parked the cart under the awning, they went into the workshop to eat, sitting amid the idle pelting equipment.

They spent the afternoon going through the tasks that would become Wayne's daily routine: watering, fixing cages, walking the fence line, maintaining the feed cart and mowing the ditches. Only breeding in spring and pelting in fall interrupted the routine. During fishing season, Wayne finished the day by taking the C60 Chevrolet to the fishery, picking up the tullibee catch and bringing it to the ranch, where he would grind the fish whole, mix in bone meal and fill the feed tank.

Some days, he stopped at the Number Two before heading home.

The Number Two was a log saloon built on a spit made from the town's trash. The part connected to the shoreline was in *dry* Roseau County, and the end that jutted into the lake with the saloon on it was in *wet* Lake of the Woods County. One January day, Wayne stopped in after spending several hours thawing out the watering system for a section of sheds. A ferocious northwest wind carried the cracking and thundering of the lake through the log walls. It took both hands to push the door closed. When he turned around and approached the bar, a group of women started laughing.

One of them pinched her nose in an exaggerated gesture. "My god, that smell is awful. What happened to you? Did you fall into a pile of horseshit with a dead skunk at the bottom?" She shook her head, her blond hair fanning out over her shoulders.

He slid the next stool closer to her and sat down. "No, I was rolling in money." He put his hat on the bar. "The problem is it doesn't start out smelling too good." She shifted her hips on her stool and turned away from her friends. He took a cigarette paper and a pinch of tobacco from his pocket.

"And what do you do to make it smell better?" She smiled and picked up her beer.

"You know my family business." He turned his attention to the rolling paper. "Weren't you in the class behind me at school?"

"I was. I'm Lindsey Muller—in case you don't remember." She leaned toward him, her blue eyes bright and her breath flammable. "Tell me about what you did while you were away."

Her friends had formed their own little group at the end of the bar. He told her about hockey and college and Alaska and Dad yelling at him. To Wayne it sounded like a recitation of failure, but to her it must have sounded like a grand adventure. There was a long pause while he rolled another cigarette.

"So, what now, Mr. Wayne Brennan who can turn mink shit into money?" She gave his shoulder a push and arched her back. Her breasts strained against the thick sweater she wore. He licked the rolling paper and sealed it, then took out his lighter and passed the tip of the cigarette through the flame.

"I'll work for my dad until I figure out what to do next or he gives me the business." After putting the lighter down, he inhaled and blew a smoke ring, which floated over her left shoulder.

"It sounds like he gives you the business already."

One of her friends said they were going home. It was a weeknight, was she coming with them? She looked back and forth and told Wayne she had to go. He tore his tab in half and handed her the scrap of paper with a pen. She studied the pen and paper for a moment, glancing at her friends. A couple of them shrugged and smiled.

She shook her head and grinned as she scribbled. "I'll probably regret this, but here."

It took him about four days to memorize her number. He dialed it every day. There isn't a lot to do in Worland during winter, so they met again in the Number Two. On the weekend, they went to the Fox Theater to see *Cat on a Hot Tin Roof.* It felt good to hold her hand and experience a warm climate, if only on the big screen. Soon they started to do what people in a small town who are bored and wildly attracted to one another do. Their favorite place was the unfinished second story of the ranch building. Afterward, she would trace the dotted line around his neck and say, "If you ever throw me over, I'll follow these instructions." Then she'd laugh and give him a poke on the sternum. By spring, her coat had taken on the mink smell too.

They got married in September. I couldn't go to the wedding—I was serving in Germany. Lance missed it too, on account of a business trip to India for Global Grain.

Before Lindsey and Wayne got into the car to leave for their honeymoon, Dad pulled Wayne aside.

"I'm glad you decided to stay. When Pete gets back, I'll be able to rely on both of you to run things."

"I didn't." Finishing sentences was difficult. He'd had a lot to drink and felt like he was floating.

"You didn't what?"

"I didn't *decide* to stay. That's merely the way it turned out."

They spent their wedding night in a ditch near Thief River Falls. Wayne fell asleep at the wheel, catching himself in time to avoid a telephone pole. They did eventually make it to the Black Hills for their honeymoon. After that, they moved into the newly finished second floor apartment in the ranch building. William was born seven months later, in the middle of breeding season.

Wayne looked down. His boot rasped on the hospital room floor.

"It's us," I said.

"What do you mean?"

"Lance is gone. Mary's going off to college." I shifted to face him. "We're it. Dad's going to give the businesses to us."

"We don't own shit. And don't think for a minute Dad wouldn't put Lance in charge."

"Why would he do that?"

"Sir Lancelot finished college. We didn't. Dad trusts him."

"And you don't?"

"It's not that I don't trust him. The thing is, I don't think Lance wants anything to do with us. He never comes back. Didn't bother to come to my wedding. Mom and Dad did a great job motivating him to get out of here."

"I love Worland. I love working outdoors in the sun with wind on my face, hearing the cry of seagulls, no matter how hard Dad pushes me. Lance can have the Cities and a big office and travel the world. All I wanted was to be a good fisherman and prove to Dad I could overcome my limitations and run the fishing business. Now I don't know if I'll even be able to walk out of this room."

Wayne said he'd wanted to play professional hockey, and when that was over, to be an engineer. Instead, someone knocked his teeth out and made him so dizzy he couldn't think. Now he had a wife, a son and twenty-thousand minks to look after. He didn't have plans. His life had turned into shit that happened and what he did about it.

"I'll tell you this much," he said. "I want us to own the businesses and not have Dad, Lance or some politicians in St. Paul fuck everything up."

I asked him why he wasn't with Mom, Dad and Mary when I came out of surgery the night before. He said he lost an hour figuring out why the feed cart wouldn't start. He'd finished feeding late and was fuming after wasting the morning and missing lunch, so he stopped at the Number Two for a whiskey.

Vern Gagnon, the owner, set the shot down and asked if he wanted a beer chaser.

"Why the hell not."

He picked up a worn newspaper from the Cities. The bar was empty. A few people scattered at the tables were having quiet conversations. He read the paper and finished his drinks. Vern asked if he wanted anything else.

"I'll have a double and a pack of Zig-Zags." Sunrays streamed in the small windows. He wanted another bracer and a smoke before going home. Lindsey and Will were probably napping.

The conversations halted at the sound of Swede Carlsen's plane flying over low. Vern put the glass and cigarette papers on the bar. "It's early for Swede to be coming back."

"You know who he's hauling around today?" Wayne started rolling a cigarette on the bar.

"A couple of builders from Connecticut. They were in here last night. I guess they restore old houses in New England. They don't know shit about fishing, but Cal outfitted them. I'm sure the old man wanted them to have an experience they wouldn't forget before selling them some windows."

"Don't worry. Swede'll give them a steep climb over the trees on Buffalo Point. Dad says he was a hell of a pilot in the war."

Worland's workers started coming in. A couple of Lindsey's friends looked in his direction and headed for a table. The sound of voices, chairs scraping, and music swirled around the room. After another double and two beers, he barely registered the phone ringing behind the bar. Vern picked up the receiver.

"Number Two, Vern speaking." He looked up at the neon clock over the bar. "Hi Lindsey, let me—"

Wayne waved his arms and shook his head. Vern raised his right hand and nodded. "Sure. I'll tell him if I see him." He hung up the receiver.

"Let me guess, she's mad and wants me to come home right away."

"You're half-right. She's mad, but you need to get to the hospital. Pete messed up his leg on the lake. Swede brought him in from Buffalo Point."

"What happened? How bad is it?"

"She didn't say. She was upset more than angry. Your folks are already there." He saw the judgment in Vern's eyes—a drunk, a wasted talent, incapable.

"I'm sure it's nothing. A couple stitches or a pulled muscle. I guess I should get going." He put his money on the bar and stood up. His legs were wobbly. The floor tilted, and he lost his balance. He grabbed at the stool, which crashed to the floor with him.

"You okay?" Vern got him back on his feet. He brushed the grit off his pants.

"I'm fine. Just lost my balance. It happens once in a while."

Wayne barely made it to the door. His bladder felt so backed-up he swore he tasted piss. In the short hallway to the toilets, he had to hold onto the wall, shuffling foot by foot to get there without letting go. Once inside, he went into the stall, turned to sit and jerked his pants down. His head hit the wall before his ass hit the seat.

Half an hour later, Vern found him slumped in the stall, groggy. Lindsey drove him home without saying a word.

Wayne pointed to the welt over his left eye. "Well, Saint Peter, that's what happened and how I got that. Sorry I didn't get here last night. Dad got on my ass about it first thing today." He stood up, grabbed the bed rail and shook it. "I better get going. A lot of hungry mink are waiting for me. And talk to that cute nurse—don't clam up and stare at the ground like you usually do."

Three: September 1960

I couldn't have stared at the ground if I'd wanted to. Flat on my back with my left leg suspended, I counted the holes in the ceiling tiles. My attempt to relieve the monotony turned monotonous. Each tile had the same number of holes. The fluorescent lights hummed. A maple branch waved outside the window. Even my pain turned dull.

As I fell into a light, drug-hazed sleep, the door closed with a metallic click. My eyes startled open. A floral scent replaced the persistent disinfectant smell. She leaned over the rail, her green eyes expanding from narrow concentration into brightness.

"Good morning Mr. Brennan."

I gazed at the side of her face, moved on to the sharp line of her jaw, down her slim neck to the nametag on her left breast, and finished at the flare of her hip. Embarrassed, and with nowhere to look, I returned to the maple branch swaying outside the window.

"Mr. Brennan, I'm nurse Vukovic. I'm here to assist with your recovery. Dr. Jensen is on his way to go over your recovery plan."

"Please call me Pete."

"I wouldn't have known it was your brother who was here earlier if he hadn't told me. There's not much resemblance."

"He's like my dad, inside and out."

"You have your mother's delicate features. I knew you were her son when they brought you in."

"What else did Wayne say?"

"He said you'd be like this."

"Like how?"

"Like you are." She rested her left hand on my forearm.

"He's full of shit." I nodded at her hand. "Did he tell you to do that?"

"No."

"Well, don't listen to what he says. He likes to stir things up."

The warmth from her palm spread into my arm in contrast to the chill in the room. "Don't worry, your mother warned me about him."

"Why isn't she looking after me?" I forced myself to face her. A gleam radiated from her smile. I couldn't look away.

"She can't, at least not here in the hospital. Staff aren't allowed to treat relatives, but trust me, as head nurse, she checks everything I do."

"Be thankful you don't work for my dad. He's a tough customer."

"Mr. Brennan, my job is to care for you."

"Please, call me Pete."

"Okay." She squeezed my forearm. "My name's Julia."

"Julia, you have beautiful eyes." It came out before I knew it.

"Did that brother of yours tell you to say that?" She withdrew and crossed her arms.

"Absolutely not."

Dr. Jensen pushed through the door, his white coat swirling around his legs. A stethoscope hung around his neck. "Pete, welcome home. I expected to run into you out on the lake or at mass, not here." He grabbed the bed rail. "You're damn lucky. You probably wouldn't have made it without Jim on board to stabilize you."

For the next half hour, he explained what would come next. Another surgery to close the amputation and prepare my leg for a prosthesis. A couple weeks to heal with stretching exercises. A few weeks to practice with the new leg, followed by several weeks learning to walk and do daily activities. Weeks and weeks and weeks, to get to what? My throat tightened. In a matter of days, I'd gone from everything possible to nothing possible.

Julia stayed after Dr. Jensen left. She put her hand back on my forearm.

"You should rest now. You've had a busy morning."

I forced myself to look at her, gripping the mattress with clenched fingers. "I grew up working on my dad's boat. That's all I ever wanted to do. I can't stand offices, and I sure as hell will never work for the Worlands." I saw myself turn into a crazy old man, sitting on the shore mending nets.

"You can go back to fishing—if you work at it. It's up to you."

"Why did you become a nurse? I don't know why anyone would want to work in a hospital."

She told me her dad worked in maintenance at the Mayo Clinic down in Rochester. One Saturday she went with him to replace some light bulbs in the emergency room. While they were there, three people from a car accident were rushed in: a couple and their little girl. Two gurneys carrying the couple burst through the doors first. A doctor shouted directions to the staff around him over the patients' moaning. A nurse walked in behind them holding bloody gauze to the right side of the girl's face. The whole thing lasted a few seconds before the medical people pushed them out. She wanted to help. She liked the excitement.

"How did you end up here—in Worland of all places?"

She lifted her hand off my arm. "We can talk about that another time. You need to rest. I'll be back this afternoon to check on you."

Julia came in twice each day to unwind the dressing, peer around at the end of my leg, and apply new bandages. In the morning, she'd write notes in a folder stored on the back of the door. Sometimes Dr. Jensen turned up to examine my leg. Every few days, they'd take the folder and retreat to the hallway to talk.

Wayne came to see me most mornings before he'd start at the mink farm. He asked more about Julia than about my recovery. Dad and Mary usually arrived together in the evening as Mom finished her shift. Mary made sketches of me lying in bed and studies of my extremities, drawings that made me glad there wasn't a mirror in the room. Dad and I talked about fishing and equipment repairs. The more we talked, the more my return to fishing seemed to move away. When we'd exhausted those subjects, he'd go on about Lance's most recent achievement. A promotion, a technical discovery, a business trip to Asia or Africa. I didn't envy Lance for his success as I think Dad did.

Lance never called the hospital to speak with me.

As Dad talked and Mary sketched, Mom would sit in a chair near the window, reading the notes in my case folder. I'd follow the early evening shadows' movement across her face. Although I held my face steady, I'm sure she could see through to my emptiness.

In the afternoon, Julia guided my legs through calisthenics. Up and down. Side to side. Various rotations. Each motion set off a different set of buzzing pulses through my muscles. I thrashed to make the sensation stop. She told me I had to stay still, somehow distract myself from the funny-bone-like sensations. I followed the sway of her hips while she took each leg through the motions. One day she noticed I had more interest in her legs than mine.

"Do you want to walk again or not?"

"I'm never going back out on the lake. How would I get around on a pitching deck? So what's the point?"

"When things would get bad for me at nursing school, my dad would tell me to stop whining. He'd say, 'Do you *really* want to be a nurse and help people, or do you want to quit and type meaningless documents, or worse, change light bulbs and clean bathrooms?' I see you, lying there in your own head, blaming yourself."

"I am not."

"You are so."

"Am not."

"Are so." She chuckled. "I've talked with your brother. He told me what happened."

"He talks too damn much, and why *are* you here? You still haven't told me. How did you end up in Worland?"

"It's my first nursing job. I eventually want to work in a trauma center, maybe in the Cities, Milwaukee or Chicago. My advisor at school said a rural hospital is the best place to get experience, and they need people. I get to deal with inpatient, emergency, surgery, all of it. Speaking of which, despite your lack of attention, your leg has healed enough to fit a prosthesis."

"Why Worland?"

"It's far enough away from home to feel on my own, yet close enough to get there in a hurry. Now let's try on some new legs."

Julia, the prosthesis salesman, and Dr. Jensen returned with legs in their arms. They set them in a pile on one of the visitor chairs. The salesman put various ones on me and took measurements. Dr. Jensen put my leg through a series of movements with each prosthesis and asked how it felt. After an hour of back-and-forth, we agreed on one. It had a beige wood shaft with a rubber foot. My stump fit into a felt-lined cup at the top. A complicated series of padded leather straps with buckles held it on. The salesman said I could use the fitting sample to learn how to put it on and walk while they made one with a custom-fitted cup in the Cities. Before he left, he said not to try to stand or walk alone—I should always have someone nearby for support.

The next day, after Julia did the routine wound check, she helped me rotate to a seated position on the side of the bed. She handed me the fitting sample. "Okay, let's see you put it on."

I fitted my stump into the cup, making sure the metal hinges lined up at the sides of my knee. I arranged the straps around my knee with the buckles landing behind my lower thigh. After fastening the buckles, I raised my arms in triumph.

"I'm ready."

"Not so fast."

"What?"

She gestured toward the floor, where the foot on the prosthesis pointed backward. "Want to try again?"

"Now you know how I lost the damn thing in the first place."

"Don't beat yourself up, honey."

I glanced up at her. "I bet you call all your patients 'honey.'"

"I don't know where that came from. It just came out." Eyes averted, she tapped the backward leg. "Now, let's get that foot pointed in the right direction."

We worked together to get the straps unbuckled. After she pulled it away, she rotated it to point the foot up. "Remember, the buckles go in front." She held the end while I redid the straps. "Keep in mind you will have to be able to do this in the dark, too."

I got the leg on with the foot pointed up. When she let go of the end, the foot thudded onto the floor. "I've got a damn baseball bat strapped on. I bet I could kick a home run."

"Before you start kicking home runs, how about if we try standing up." She sat to my left on the bed. Her soft thigh pressed into my hip bone while she took my arm. "I'll count to three. On three, you push down and rotate your knees. I'll lift you by the arm. Lean into me as we stand to hold your balance."

She pulled me up by the arm. I teetered right, then left, leaning into her. Instinctively, I shifted my weight to the right. My balance went off. I flailed my right arm to straighten up. Julia pulled me into her arms.

"I've got you. Let's just stand here a moment. Get used to the feeling of the prosthesis under your knee." Inches separated our faces. "I'm going to push you out and hold your arm. Try to sense where your balance point is. When you think you've found it, tell me."

"Listen, I can't stand on a solid stone floor. I'll never be able to stand on a pitching deck. Help me sit down."

"No, you're going to stand on your own today, if only for a few seconds. You can lie down after that."

"This is pointless."

"Do you want to get back on the boat or not?" She pushed me away while maintaining the grip on my arm. "What'll it be?"

"Let go!"

"Are you going to stand or sit?"

"Stand goddamnit!"

"Good, because you already are." Her arms hung at her sides. She smiled.

"Oh, you're tricky. What else do you have up your sleeve?"

"That's enough for today." She helped me to sit on the bed. "I have to get to the other patients. We'll work on it again tomorrow."

The maple leaves outside the window had yellow streaks when my custom leg arrived. Julia and the salesman proposed I try it on and take a few steps around the room. I'd been confined to that miserable space for over four weeks. I wanted to get the hell out of there.

"Give me that." I swung myself around to sit on the edge of the bed. "We're going out to the hallway," I said while I strapped on the new leg.

"Pete, you're not steady," Julia said.

"Sir, we need to make sure it fits correctly. Maybe we should start in here."

"Please call me Pete."

"Pete, let me quickly check the fit, and then you can run in the Olympics as far as I'm concerned." He made some slight adjustments to the straps. Over the next few minutes, he pushed, pulled and twisted the prosthesis. The last thing he did was try to push a feeler gauge in the cup. The thin metal tab hurt when it poked my sore stump. "How does it feel?"

I stood up. "Feels all right." I held my right arm out to Julia. "Let's get this show on the road."

Every day for the next four weeks we practiced walking in the hallway. The first time out of the room I barely made it past the door. The prothesis's weight hung from my thigh like a loose anchor. I overcompensated to the right and went off balance, pinning Julia between me and the wall. Her body tensed into an exquisite combination of firm and soft. We lingered there a moment longer than I expected before she pushed me back to vertical.

"Next time I expect you'll *ask* me to dance. Okay?"

"I promise, and it will be at a place with better music."

We settled into a routine of going further down the hall each day. At first she held my right arm for the entire walk. Dr. Jensen spotted us one day mid-walk and said we made a nice-looking couple. I glanced over to see her reaction—she was looking at the floor with a smile.

Another day, Julia asked about the fishing business. The maple leaves had turned bright yellow by then. I told her how my grandfather, Ciaran Brennan, set the first pound nets in Lake of the Woods. He shipped sturgeon and walleye to the best restaurants and grocers in the Cities. The business grew large enough that he convinced the Northern Pacific railway to build a spur. They sent refrigerated cars from the Cities filled with produce, and the cars went back with fish.

"Calvin Worland came with the crew building the spur. He was the lead carpenter responsible for the platform and depot. Afterward, he built stores and houses, starting the hardware and lumber business in the process."

"How did your dad get into the mink business? Didn't you say your grandfather started a fishing business?"

"I did. The mink business started by chance. My grandmother had three trained wolves. One day they bolted off into the woods. Dad was about thirteen at the time. He found them tearing apart a mink caught in a snare. An Indian boy about the same age pounced on Dad from behind, blaming him for ruining the pelt. While the two boys tussled on the ground, the wolves surrounded them."

"How did they get out of that?"

"They made a deal. Dad agreed to call off the wolves and take the Indian boy out on my grandfather's fishing boat if the boy would teach him how to snare minks. That's how my dad met Jim Thunder. They built five cages and sold the pelts in town. But they also discovered that feeding the minks fish made for lustrous pelts."

"Is he the same Jim that Dr. Jensen mentioned?"

"He is. When Dad went to college, Jim joined the Navy. He was in for twenty years. Dad calls him the Chief who made Chief."

"What did your dad study in college?"

"Mechanical engineering. He graduated from the University of Minnesota in 1931. Unemployment was nearly 20 percent. He only came back to Worland because he couldn't find a job anywhere else. His only option was to help my grandfather with the fishing business and restart the mink business. He took over the fishing business and turned those five cages into the largest mink farm in Minnesota. We have almost twenty-five thousand minks now, and the fishing operation feeds us and them."

"Do you like working for your dad?"

No one had ever asked me that. And why would they? I came back to Worland without thinking. The idea I could go somewhere else never occurred to me. My obligation to Dad and desire to return were as much a part of me as my heart and lungs. Hauling nets made me feel strong, alive. The boat heaving underneath created an exhilarating sensation like an amusement park ride— as soon as I got off, I wanted to get back on. But did I *like* working for Dad? The question hadn't occurred to me. It confounded me.

"I love being on the lake. As for Dad, I know he's doing what he thinks is best for me, but sometimes it's too much. It's hard to take it." I'd made it to the end of the hall. "Sometimes I can't take it." I told her I was tired.

"I understand. Let's get you back to your room."

Near the end of my stay in the hospital, Julia came into my room during her break. She closed the door.

"I've got to get off my feet."

Without a word, she lowered the bed rail and lay down next to me. We stared at the ceiling. I told her each tile had 225 holes. She told me she wanted to see the Rocky Mountains.

"Have you been out on the lake? I could take you."

"I haven't."

"I can't take you until spring. Dad took the boat out for winter last week."

"You're backing out already?" She nudged my arm.

"You know the jetty next to the Number Two? The view of the lake from the end is amazing. Have you walked out there? We could do that once I get out of here, although I may need some help stepping around the rocks."

"I haven't been there." She kissed me on the cheek. "I'd like that."

On the day I left the hospital, Julia pushed me in a wheelchair to the front entrance. The bare trees shivered under the gray October sky. Mom met us in the lobby and thanked Julia for all her hard work. Dad waited in his pickup under the awning. Julia opened the passenger door for me, and I introduced her to him.

On the drive home I told him I looked forward to getting back on the boat. He nodded, "She's pretty. Be careful getting tangled up with a nurse." He winked at me. "Let's see if she's got you back on your feet".

Four: May 1961

Dad and Jim stood in the boat at the bottom of the ladder. From the dock, they looked as if they were a hundred feet below. Dad guided my feet to each rung, over the gunwale and onto the deck. I held onto the gunwale while I got a sense of the boat's motion. Moose held out my lunch box from above. I reached for it, the deck tilted and I lost my balance. Jim grabbed one of my flailing arms before I fell.

"Let go. I'm fine."

"That's a hell of a start to your first day back."

"It's actually my second if you count that day last year, and I want to come back in one piece this time."

"Pete, you're the pilot." Dad handed over my lunch box. "And that's all you're doing. Now let's go."

At the first net, I sat on a fish box and watched them haul. Dad ran the dipper, maintaining perfect tension on the cable. I stood at the second net, leaning on the pilothouse to counter the five-foot swells. When the others had their backs to me, I'd step away and count to see how long I could stand on the rolling deck. Jim caught me once struggling to regain my balance.

"You might take flight if you flap any harder."

"I'll be out here flapping long after you've turned to dust."

Jim dropped the furl of net he was holding. He thrust his face to within an inch of mine. "You wouldn't be flapping at all if I hadn't saved your ass."

"I'm grateful for that, but I'll bury you. I'll be hauling nets long after you're gone."

"We'll see." Dad pushed Jim away. "The state may have something to say about that."

"What are they up to now?"

"While you were making time with that nurse, I went to St. Paul to deal with the legislature."

"What happened?"

"Remember the pound net ban they threatened me with?"

"Vaguely. What I do remember from that day is how much it hurt when Jim pulled out my belt and whipped me in the ass."

He smiled. "I should have done that before you took your damn leg off. Maybe you'd have listened better, learned faster."

Moose shrugged. "It wouldn't have helped."

"I guess I really am back. Now I wonder why I looked forward to it."

"Pete, listen. They wanted to ban pound netting. The sportos were hollering for it and the legislators were caving. I needed to throw them a bone while this trawler business played out. I suggested a commercial license ban, and they went for it. Now I can't sell my license to you, and you can't inherit it."

"Dad! Why did you do that?"

"I had no choice! If I hadn't, they would have put us out of business. It buys us time. They also agreed to a four-year study of the trawler's effect. If the fish population declines, the trawler experiment is finished."

"I saved some money in the Army. Maybe if you started to pay me, I could buy my own damn license."

"That's not an option. No new licenses either. I'm counting on the trawler to have a negative effect. Maybe I can get them to reverse the transfer ban later. After all, a little small business lobbying goes a long way."

"What about paying me?"

"What about it?"

"You're paying Wayne."

"He has a family, but sometimes I wonder why I do pay him. One day he does everything and more, and the next I find him sitting in the hay shed with a beer staring at the top of his boots. Anyway, while you're under my roof, you'll work for it."

"I'll have a family soon. I'm marrying Julia."

"Does she know that?" Jim huffed.

"She does. I proposed last Saturday. I had to do it without a ring, but she said yes anyway. I promised I'd get her one later."

"I've been all over the world. The generosity of women never ceases to amaze me."

Moose took off his cap and scratched his head. "I thought you said she was smart."

"Congratulations son." Dad held out his flask. "I'll help you get that ring."

We passed the whiskey around. Moose and Jim shook my hand and patted me on the back. As soon as Dad returned the flask to his pocket, he told us to get back to work.

On the way back to Worland, I used the two channel markers on the south side of the river as a guide. They're thirty feet tall with a black and white diamond in the center of a wood frame. A red beacon flashes from the top of each marker. I lined up the markers to navigate into the Worland River channel. The diamonds make them look like knights holding up their shields, bracing themselves against an invisible force.

Five: November 1962

Lance walked between Dad and me. He paid no attention to Wayne on the feed cart, appearing and disappearing from the sheds. It didn't take long for my leg to start aching. When Dad asked me to come with him that Thanksgiving morning, I knew traipsing along the rutted paths of the mink farm would make my stump raw for a week. Lance hadn't been back in seven years, and he looked over the place as if he were in a foreign country.

"How many this year?"

Dad stopped next to a rut full of snowmelt and cage runoff. "About twenty-five thousand. It gets bigger every year. Jacqueline Kennedy and Marilyn Monroe wore our fur. We need to build more sheds." From the gleam in his eyes, I could tell he saw the imagined sheds on the east end of the property. If he did decide to expand, feeding the additional animals would put more pressure on the fishing business—and me.

"We could barely catch enough tullibees for mink feed." I stepped in front of Lance so the three of us formed a small triangle on a patch of snow. "We had nets at the fish runs off Buffalo Point *and* Springsteel Island. If the state continues to allow trawlers, we're going to be in trouble."

"What about walleyes and sturgeon?" For the first time, Lance looked at me like I was someone to be treated seriously.

I wished I could have given him better news. "Prices were good last year, but the catch was smaller. Size was down too. Has been the last couple years." I felt relief after saying it out loud. The higher prices compensated for the decreased volume. Still, the direction of the business didn't feel good. If the catch got too small, price wouldn't matter. Lance's eyes narrowed. He'd picked up my concern despite my effort to hide it.

"How do you plan on dealing with the trend?" His feet were constantly moving, compacting the snow. "Dad, are you going back to the legislature? Do you think you can end this trawler business? How are the other fishermen doing?"

"The other operations are slowly going bankrupt. Without mink to generate real revenue, there's no money in fishing." He glanced up at the letters on the side of the building. "Most of them are leaving fishing to work in the Worland window factory. We've got to convince the legislature to ban trawlers. I'm counting on the population study to confirm what we're seeing."

"How many are we pelting this year?"

"Twenty thousand. Starting tomorrow."

"Pete, how are you holding up? You've looked uncomfortable since we got here. Are you getting used to it?"

"I get around the boat okay." My leg hurt like a son of a bitch after the walking we'd done, but I refused to complain. With Lance showing me some respect, I couldn't allow myself to crack in front of him. I want him to see I'd recovered and could fully participate in the business if Dad put him in charge. "Dad and Jim took it easy on me. I piloted the boat at first. Near the end of the season, I lifted and ran the dipper as well."

"How does it feel to be a married man?"

"Great! I panicked a little after we got back from the honeymoon. With both of us working, we lived in a mess. Since fishing season, I've had a chance to get the house squared away. She's not happy today though. We'd planned on spending a quiet morning together. Instead, she's helping Mom get dinner ready."

Dad patted me on the back. "I'm sorry, Pete. It's not every day that I get the chance to walk around the operation with my sons. I'm sure you'll make it up to her."

"Welcome to marriage, little brother! How was the honeymoon? I heard you went out west."

"We went to Yellowstone and the Tetons. She loved the mountains and Old Faithful."

The feed cart emerged from a shed in the distance. Wayne drove toward us. His eyes narrowed as he got closer. Lance was asking Dad about pelt prices, and they weren't paying any attention to the approaching feed cart. Wayne was about twenty yards away when our eyes met. He accelerated through a filthy puddle and hit us with a five-foot-high splash.

Wayne's laughter echoed off the tin roofs. Lance flapped his arms to shake off the sludge.

"Time you got some mud on your armor, Sir Lancelot," Wayne hollered as he drove toward the gas pump.

"Goddamnit!" Lance stomped his feet to shake off his pants.

I laughed and wiped the muck off my face. Lance had been away too long. He'd lost his edge, as well as his sense of humor. A prank wouldn't have bothered him when we were kids. He'd have calmly plotted his revenge, and the next day Wayne would have fish heads or mink shit in the toes of his shoes. When Lance was a kid, the idea of getting away from Worland gave him strength. It appeared to me his patience with us and our way of life had run out.

Dad pulled off his hat, shook it, then put it back on his head. A grin crept onto his face. "You're not in the Cities anymore."

I slapped my pant legs to knock off the chunks of grime. Lance lowered the bill of his cap. He pulled on his shirt collar.

"There's shit running down my back."

In the distance, Wayne hopped off the feed cart. While he waited for the gas tank to fill, he jumped up and down, flapping his arms with a big smile on his face.

Lance collected himself. "He hasn't changed a bit. Did you get any tattoos while you were in the Army?"

I didn't want to explain myself to Lance. "No, Wayne's the tattoo man. Although I think you should get one of a boot mark on your ass.

Maybe it'll remind you where you're from." I shoved his shoulder. He had to put one foot in the gunk to maintain his balance. He smiled and put his foot back on the snow patch.

Dad leaned in between us. "Don't get your mother started on tattoos. Okay?"

Wayne pulled the nozzle out of the feed cart and hung it on the gas pump. He drove off toward another section of sheds.

Lance turned to me. "Are you mending nets now?"

"Yes, we left them in too long and the ice tore them up. We got them out before they would've been a total loss. Moose nearly died when we were pulling up stakes. He fell into the drink, and we couldn't get to him. Had to use the winch to haul him out. He was nearly hypothermic when we got in."

"Dad, do you have insurance?"

"Insurance is for pessimists."

I agreed. To buy insurance is to hand money to a corporation for nothing. They don't make money by paying claims.

We walked into a shed. On either side of us were minks scurrying about in their cages. What light there was came in at our feet and through the rotating ventilators, which created a strobe effect.

I watched two minks chase each other until they formed a brown blur. They suddenly stopped and looked at me as if they knew what was going to happen the next day.

Dad patted Lance on the shoulder. "Does Gwen want a coat? I can put you in touch with a furrier in New York."

"Always the salesman, huh Dad?"

"Think Mink." He grinned. "She'd look great in a sapphire coat."

Lance nodded. "Business must be good."

"You have no idea. I'll show you when we review the ledger."

Reviewing the numbers after Thanksgiving dinner was a ritual. When we turned sixteen, Dad taught me and my brothers two lessons: how to fire his old Remington shotgun and the mysteries of double-entry bookkeeping. From then on, he treated us like adults and expected us to act like it. He took us hunting and discussed the state of the business. Since I'd learned to read the financial statements, Lance and Wayne had been away. It would be the first time we reviewed them together. Trawlers and taking on debt worried me. My aching leg reminded me that merely walking presented a challenge, a challenge I'd slowly accepted, yet served as reminder that things could go wrong at any moment.

At the same time, standing there in the muck, I had something bigger on my mind—fatherhood.

Six: November 1962

Back home, I found Julia sitting at the kitchen table staring into a cup of black coffee. Dark circles hung below her eyes. The tails of her gravy-splattered shirt dangled over her waist. I kissed her on the cheek. She pushed me away so hard I nearly fell into the chair next to her.

"You smell awful. What happened?"

"One of Wayne's pranks."

"You want to tell me about it?"

"Not really. How did it go at Mom and Dad's?"

"My God, sweetie, when I got over there they had just woke up. And your mom is right. That Gwen sure is a piece of work."

"You want to tell me about it?"

Julia started with the turkey bobbing in the kitchen sink. Mom had touched the bird to check if it was ready for stuffing. It spun around like an unmoored boat, making a hollow clunk each time it bounced off the side. Mom had told Julia it was after ten-thirty by the time the supper dishes were put away and she got the turkey out of the freezer.

Mom lifted it out of the water and set it in the roasting pan. The wrapping came off easily. A low hum from the refrigerator periodically broke the stillness in the house. Her fingers searched the chest cavity for the giblets. As she pulled out the neck, Mary shuffled into the kitchen, her slippers rasping on the floor.

"Good morning, sweetie. How are you?"

"Good morning, Mom. Hi, Julia. I don't feel very good."

Mary's sleep-mangled hair reminded Julia of a tufted titmouse, the way it stood up on the top of her head. She lifted her arms and hugged Mom.

"What's wrong?"

"I couldn't get to sleep, then I kept waking up. How are you?"

"Tired from thawing the turkey."

Mom had spent the night rotating the bird and changing its watery bed every hour as if it were a debilitated patient.

"Do you want something to settle your stomach?" Mom asked. Mary smelled like oil and cigarettes; the color seemed leached out of her skin. She looked more sad than sick.

"Would you like some coffee?" Julia offered.

"I think I'll sit for a minute." Mary lowered herself into the chair between the round breakfast table and the corner of the kitchen. Her pale skin stood out against the green and black tile wainscoting.

Mom split the heart into eight pieces. Julia chopped the fibrous neck into disks. Mary stood up and walked to the metal breadbox. She pulled out two slices and put them in the toaster.

"Sweetie, please leave the bread out. I'll use it for the stuffing."

"Do you want me to start cubing it?"

"No. Please sit down and relax. I'll bring over your toast when it's done."

She slumped back into the wood chair. "I'm going to sit in Dad's place. He never let me sit here as a kid."

The old chair creaked as she struggled to find a comfortable position. I knew it well. We never sat in it. There was a shine on the top of the armrests from years of polishing by Dad's flannel shirts. None of the other kitchen chairs had armrests.

Mom finished cutting the neck, slicing each disk into four pieces. Julia took two cups down from the cupboard. She poured the coffee and set Mary's in front of her. With a morning in the kitchen ahead, she drank the entire cup—and part of another. Julia usually drank half of what she poured for herself, and I'd drink the rest before heading to the boat.

"How are your classes going?" Mom asked.

"I'm not sure if being a painter is the right thing for me." Mary held her hands over the steaming liquid like it was an open fire.

The liver cut easily. It virtually fell apart into two dozen brown blobs. Mary's toast popped up. It was charred, the way Dad liked it. Mom held the pieces up, one in each hand to show Mary.

"Don't worry Mom. It's okay. I'll eat it."

"You sure? I don't know why he likes it this way. It tastes like ashes, and crumbs go everywhere, which I get to clean up from under the table."

"I've gotten used to eating things I don't like at school."

Mom reached into the cupboard and grabbed a small plate. "The usual?"

Mary nodded. "Tell me again how you decided to be a nurse."

Mom retrieved the peanut butter and grape jelly from a cabinet below the counter. "I'll put lots of peanut butter on."

Mary fidgeted in the chair while Mom spread the peanut butter and jelly. Mom gave her the toast, then sipped her coffee. Julia collected the giblets on the cutting board into a pile.

"I became a nurse so I could be independent. Back in the twenties, teaching and nursing were the only professional jobs available to women, and Grandpa Fox insisted I be educated." Mom started to cube the bread. "Otherwise, I would've had to work as a maid or a waitress or something like that. I certainly wasn't ready to get married."

Mary tore a corner off a piece of her toast. Crumbs sprayed onto her lap. "That's not true. Amelia Earhart flew airplanes. Look at Georgia O'Keefe. There were women doctors, lawyers and artists back then." She brushed the crumbs off her lap onto the floor.

"They were rare. I was fourteen when women got the vote. Being a doctor or a lawyer was not realistic for me. I wanted to manage myself and my money and not have to depend on anyone. I wanted to live in a city near the ocean. I dreamed of living in Seattle or Boston with a man who looked like Gary Cooper. Your father wanted to live in Seattle, too." Mom gathered the cubed bread into a pile.

The coffee was not working as well as Julia had hoped. She'd worked a night shift the day before. A headache pulsed behind her eyes, and her arms required conscious commands to move.

Mary finished chewing and looked up from her plate. "Why did you want to leave?"

"I wanted to be someplace with energy. See things I'd read about. Back then, I believed dreams could come true. Some people grow up in the city wanting to see the country. I grew up in the country wanting to see the city. When I went to Winnipeg for nursing school, I thought I'd never come back."

Mary held her cup on the sides with both hands and lifted it to her mouth. She squinted like a gunfighter ready to dispatch a hapless opponent.

"Why *did* you come back?"

"Is that an accusation or a question? It was a world of limited opportunity. There was no air travel, no television. We didn't have the pill. Then the economy crashed. I gave up on dreams. You found small satisfactions, or none at all."

Julia said she sensed a gap opening between them. Their shared experience diminished by the changing times.

Mom started to cube the bread as if she wanted to kill it.

"I graduated from nursing school at the start of the Depression. Unless you knew someone or were willing to compromise yourself, it was practically impossible for a single woman to find a job. Men were given priority, and I didn't have the will, after all the work to finish college, to establish myself in a new city. Times were hard enough. My only choice was to come back. I waited two years to get hired at the hospital. Before that, I volunteered whenever they needed help. I met your father while I was waiting to get hired."

The coffee started to work on Mary. She became more animated.

"I love this story. Mom, tell Julia how you met Dad."

"I have to say first that I did actually know Arthur in high school, but we didn't have anything to do with each other. Anyway, on a sweltering July afternoon, I walked with Grandpa Fox to the fishery. Usually, Johnny LeBeau cleaned and weighed the fish after Arthur and Grandpa Brennan unloaded the boat, but Johnny was sick, so your dad was there. I hadn't seen him in four years, not since I left for Winnipeg. As soon as I walked, in it felt like he owned the place. I remember the stink and the dribbling of melting ice. Grandpa asked for two walleyes. Arthur buried his arm in an ice-filled wooden box and searched around, then pulled out a two-foot-long fish as if it were a rabbit from a hat.

'How's that?' he said and stood with his shoulders back and a broad smile. Something about his confidence and the way he magically produced that fish made me want to know him better.

'We'll take it,' I said, ignoring Grandpa, who said they didn't need such a large fish. From then on, I volunteered every Friday to get fish for dinner. Grandpa warned me to stay away from the Brennans. He said they were bogtrotters and drunks who lived with wolves. The truth is, we're all bogtrotters with the soggy land around here. Your father hooked me when he said fishing is a special vocation. It wasn't his chosen profession—he was pulled into it and was good at it. He believes it's sacred because St. Peter was a fisherman. It was honest work in desperate times. I could tell he was a man who took commitments seriously."

"Dad doesn't smile much these days." Mary pushed the half-eaten toast around her plate without picking it up.

"Neither do you. You've been moping around since you got here. Are you sure you're okay? You've barely touched your breakfast."

"Mom, I'm fine. I have a lot on my mind. I have a big art project to finish before Christmas and an economics test next week, that's all."

Julia said tension oozed from her voice. Mom finished slicing the bread, heaping it in a pile of cubes next to the giblets on the cutting board. Mary probably felt worse than she let on. Dad was the same way. When he didn't feel well, he pushed on until he collapsed, rather than admit fallibility.

"Maybe a couple aspirin will help." Mary dangled a piece of toast over her mouth before taking a bite. Mom opened a small drawer next to the silverware. She pulled out a clear bottle, which she handed to Mary.

"Have you seen Eddie?"

"I've seen him a couple times. We went to a football game last month." She dumped two white pills into her hand.

"How is he?"

Her mouth turned down while she swallowed the aspirin. "He's fine. He's busy with school and his fraternity. Can we talk about something else?"

"Okay."

"When is everyone coming over?"

"I told them to come at two. The turkey should be ready by three. Arthur and Lance are at the mink farm with Wayne and Pete. Wayne is giving the mink their last supper. Do you want to make the pies after you get dressed?"

"Sure."

Mary padded off to her room. The kitchen returned to its morning tranquility, broken only by the refrigerator hum. Mom turned on the oven to preheat it for the turkey. A small group of chickadees landed on the frozen clothesline in the yard. Occasionally one would dart over to the bird feeder to quickly peck at the black sunflower seeds, then dart back to the line. Julia watched them fly back and forth; thankful she didn't have to scour the barren landscape for her meals. She tipped the cutting board and scraped the bread cubes and giblets into a bowl. The chickadees flew in a swarm out over the field behind the shed until they were absorbed by the white landscape. Using a long wooden spoon, she stirred the giblets and bread together. Mom chopped two onions. Tears ran down her face.

"My last one has left home."

Real tears mixed with those from the onion. Julia dumped in the chopped pieces, and added salt and sage, then slowly stirred the mixture.

Gwen came into the kitchen a few minutes later, as Mom was taking a bag of potatoes out from under the sink. She went straight to the percolator without saying hello, while Mom set the potatoes next to the breakfast table. Her large belly, indigo maternity dress and black hair made her look like a walking blueberry. Leaning against the counter, she poured a half cup of coffee and added an equal amount of cream.

"Mind if I make some eggs?"

"Sit. I'll make them. You should stay off your feet," Mom said.

"Thank you. I can peel potatoes or cut vegetables if you want help."

"Okay." Julia could tell Gwen expected Mom to say she didn't need help. "How do you like your eggs?"

"Sunny side up."

That was as far from Gwen's personality as you could get. On a break at the hospital one day, Mom had told Julia she liked Gwen well enough. She was smart. Mom admired her ambition. What she didn't like was the way she treated Lance. When she had visited them in Boston for graduation, Gwen had ordered him around like a servant. Mom said she hardly got to talk with him because he was always fetching food or cleaning some already spotless surface at her command. Gwen gave off the impression she expected disaster to strike at any moment due to the incompetence of everyone around her.

Mom handed Gwen the potato peeler. She looked at it as if Mom had handed her a knife and asked her to cut her own throat.

"I hate peeling potatoes. My mother used to make me do it with a straight bladed knife. I eat them with the skin on now."

Gwen didn't have to peel potatoes. I bet Mom wanted to see if she would refuse. Julia said she looked like she couldn't decide if her in-laws were beneath her or not. The fact they were so much alike probably threw off the scale Gwen used to determine how to treat people.

Mom placed a four-quart pot in front of Gwen and a twelve-quart pot half filled with water to her right. Gwen took a potato from the bag and started to peel. Mom put the plate with Gwen's eggs on the table.

"You should eat first. Your eggs will get cold."

She put down the potato and the peeler without looking up.

"What is it you don't like about me?"

Gwen's right hand moved to pick up the fork on the plate.

"It's not that I don't like you. In fact, I admire what you've done. I just wish Lance came home more often and I suspect you're the reason he doesn't."

Gwen stabbed the tines into the yolk. "I've never stopped him from coming here." She lifted a limp piece of egg white to her mouth.

Mom removed three pie crusts from the freezer and set them on the counter to thaw. "I'm sure you haven't stopped him *directly*."

"Ginny, I understand you being upset about having to come out east for our wedding, but—"

"No, you don't understand." Mom pulled three cans of pie filling from the pantry and placed them next to the pie crusts. "You have no idea how difficult that was for us. We begged you to have the wedding here. Pete had left for the Army. Mary was starting her senior year of high school. Wayne had been back from the Air Force only a short time. But you refused. You knew Wayne and Mary couldn't come because they would have to stay here to watch the mink farm."

Julia began to stuff the turkey. She had to resist saying out loud that she wanted to do to Gwen what she was doing to the turkey.

"That's not true. I did understand." Gwen waved the potato peeler as she spoke. "We wanted a small ceremony and a fresh start in a neutral place."

"Why did you come back now?"

"Lance promised Arthur we'd come for Thanksgiving last winter when he was in St. Paul dealing with the fishing regulations. Also, I wanted to see where Lance came from after hearing so much about it. Once the baby arrives in December, I won't be able to travel for a while."

Mary trudged into the kitchen wearing jeans and a plaid shirt, her tuft held down by a tortoiseshell headband. Some of her color had returned. Julia finished stuffing the turkey.

"How did you sleep?" Mary asked Gwen.

"I fell asleep right away. Then sometime in the middle of the night, the smell of Lance's mink farm coat woke me up. We had to endure that smell all day yesterday in the car. I don't know why—it wasn't in the room—but it got into my head." Gwen allowed the potato she'd finished peeling to plop into the pot.

Mom pointed at Gwen. "That smell paid for Lance's education."

"Touché." Gwen flung the potato skin into the smaller pot.

"Lance has come a long way. Arthur and I were determined that at least one of you would be educated and get out of here."

"Think I'll make it out, Mom?"

"You will if you learn a practical skill, sweetie."

Mom had told Julia she worried about Mary studying painting. She wanted her daughter to be comfortable, and art doesn't pay the bills. Mary had done beautiful paintings of Dad and me working on the lake—they hung in Dad's office. Mom had told me she'd often found Dad staring at the pictures, lost in thought when he was supposed to be preparing invoices.

Gwen pulled a couple small peels off the back of her hands. "What do you think of our Irish president?"

Mary started to sing. "Hap-py Birth-day *Mis-ter Pres-i-dent*—did you see that?"

"That Marilyn Monroe was a piece of work." Mom dried her hands.

Mary shifted in her chair. "He's *very* handsome."

Gwen leaned forward to hold a potato over the small pot. "During the missile crisis, I kept seeing myself pregnant and trying to run to a fallout shelter. After the first couple days, I gave up on the idea and decided I would sit on a lawn chair in the front yard and watch the missiles arrive."

"We were prepared at the hospital," Mom said. "Beds and equipment were ready in the basement, but I don't know how anyone would have gotten there."

Gwen's pessimistic cloud was expanding in the kitchen. Julia needed a diversion. It was too depressing to tell them the rest, which was that the hospital preparation was theater more than anything else. Something to do to pass the time until the end came. Julia was glad to do it. She had told me it kept her mind off the idea that the world as we knew it might disappear twenty minutes from any given moment.

Mom put the turkey in the oven, setting the timer for fifteen minutes. She asked Julia to baste the turkey when the timer went off.

"Ready to start the pies, Mary? I thought I'd try those new frozen crusts, see if they're any good."

Gwen continued peeling potatoes. "My mother made great pies from scratch. It's one of the few things I remember about her."

Mom turned to Gwen. "You can make crusts from scratch if you want. I have all the ingredients."

The last potato splashed into the large pot. "My mother died before she could teach me her baking secrets. There's no way frozen will be as good as homemade."

Julia jerked her shirt tails out of her jeans to keep herself quiet.

Mary stood up and came over to the counter. "What do we do?"

"It's simple. Roll out the crust, lay it in a tin, and pour in the filling."

"Mom, you sound like a TV commercial."

"Guilty as charged, sweetie."

Gwen came over to the sink to wash her hands. "I'm going to take a nap." She dried her hands and left the kitchen. They waited for the sound of the bedroom door closing.

"What was it like to ride all the way up here with her in Lance's little car?" Mom rolled out one of the crusts and draped it over a pie tin.

Mary picked up a crust and examined it like it was a rare object. "I'm not looking forward to the ride back."

"Did you talk to her much?"

"We talked a lot, actually. She likes rock 'n' roll music. Believes in women's liberation. You know, we shouldn't be subservient to men and all that. Full equality and have control of our lives."

Mom leaned on the counter. "At school, I met women who thought we should be treated equally to men, but they never said 'liberation,' as if we were in some sort of prison. I believe in women's equality, although I didn't feel like I needed liberating. Did she talk about her folks, or where she grew up?"

"I didn't know growing up on a dairy farm was so rough. She had to milk cows, collect eggs and help raise sheep. There weren't any other kids nearby to play with. Then her mother died of ovarian cancer at forty-one. Her dad started to drink after that, and he sent her away to boarding school."

Mom put the last crust in a tin. "Cows are a lot different than mink. They're not vicious. Did she have any advice for getting through school?"

"Not really. Study hard and stay out of trouble."

The timer went off and Julia basted the turkey. Mary seemed nervous and content at the same time. She poured filling into the pie crusts, laughing as they each dipped a finger into the last one. Mary said she had to do some economics reading for an upcoming final and left the kitchen.

"I'm going to be too tired to eat," Mom said.

It was around 11:30 when Julia left Mom and Dad's. She'd been home for an hour when I came in from the mink farm and found her sitting at the kitchen table.

She laid her head on the cool tabletop. "This feels nice." Her eyelids drooped until they covered her eyes. I asked how she was doing.

"I think we should go see my parents next Thanksgiving."

Seven: November 1962

Mom and Dad's house smelled of roast turkey. Will toddled around the living room with Wayne holding the boy's hands to steady him. The front door hadn't even closed before he started in on me.

"Saint Peter! I think he'll walk better than you pretty soon."

Julia squeezed my hand until my fingers hurt.

"I'm sure he'll skate like his old man in no time," I said.

That little boy scared the hell out of me. It was hard to miss how helpless he was, and how poorly equipped I felt to take care of the one we had coming. Julia released her grip.

"I love that little wool cap he's wearing. I wish I could sleep in one of those."

"You're beautiful without a cute cap."

Lindsey took Will's hands from Wayne and led him down the hall to Mom and Dad's bedroom for a nap. Mom waved us to the dining room table. "Sit where you like, no assigned places."

Lance and Lindsey returned from the hallway one after the other, and Mom disappeared into the kitchen while we sat down. Dad came out of the kitchen carrying a broad blade knife and a sharpening steel. He sat down at the head of the table. Mom carried out the turkey in a steel roaster. Placing the end of the sharpening steel on a cutting board, Dad honed the knife, drawing the blade slowly half a dozen times across the shaft. He reached into his back pocket and took out a blue handkerchief he used to wipe his nose, raising it to wipe the blade. Mom paused in the middle of taking off her apron, a horrified look on her face.

"Arthur, stop that." She sat down to his left, giving him a mock-stern look.

"I was wondering if anyone was going to speak up." Dad put his handkerchief away and instead wiped the knife with a white cloth for removing metal filings. "Who's going to say grace?"

"I will." And Mom began.

"Bless us, O Lord,

And these thy gifts, which we are about to receive,

From thy bounty.

Through Christ our Lord."

"Amen," we replied, and arranged our napkins.

Mom held her hands together. "And thanks for bringing Mary, Lance and Gwen here safely."

Dad carved the bird. The serving bowls and a bottle of whiskey made their journeys around the table. Mom interrupted Wayne with a scoop of mashed potatoes hovering above his plate. "Please do up the top button on your shirt."

"Come on, Mom."

I had the urge to giggle. My hand shook, causing the spoonful of corn I held to dribble onto my plate. Mom glanced at me and then Wayne.

"I don't want to see that tattoo. Not today."

Lindsey leaned into Wayne. "I think it makes you look dangerous."

"How do you know I'm *not* dangerous?" Wayne kissed her. He turned to Mom and pushed the top button of his shirt through the hole with a flourish.

Mom put her hands palm down on either side of her plate. "Thank you."

The dish with the turkey was the last to make its way around. When it returned to Dad, he set it next to his plate.

"Does everyone have what they want?"

Wayne waved the bulbous end of a drumstick. "Yes." His eyes settled on me. "Saint Peter, I believe this leg is too short to be yours."

Julia grabbed my hand.

"It looks perfect for you," I said. "I think you should start eating." He took a large bite, finishing by slurping in a long piece of skin.

Dad waited for Wayne to put the drumstick back on his plate. He held up his shot glass. "*Sláinte*." We took up our whiskeys, touched glasses and drank together.

Wayne slammed his glass down. "So, tell us what's happening in the Cities." He looked back and forth between Lance and Mary. "What wonders are we missing?"

Mary set her shot glass on the table. "They're building a highway right through the center." She picked up her fork. "It's terrible. Neighborhoods divided. People losing their houses."

"Glad we don't have that nonsense around here." Wayne shoveled in a spoonful of potatoes. "These are good, Mom."

"Gwen made them. She was very helpful this morning." Mom looked at Gwen, who glared back with narrow eyes.

Lance finished chewing on a wing and set the bone on his plate. "Once the highway is done, it will take only a few minutes to get to St. Paul from Minneapolis."

"I'd have thought you'd want to spend *more* time in your hip little car." Mary mixed the things on her plate together with listless strokes.

Gwen used a knife and fork to corral some peas. "It was awful getting to St. Kate's from our house yesterday. Took almost two hours. You know Mary, you should come out to Deephaven and see us. It would do you good to get out of St. Paul occasionally. There's a little beach we can walk to. Maybe you could help me paint the baby's room some weekend."

Mary twisted in her chair and shrugged. "Yeah, maybe." She looked at me for rescue. "What happened out at the ranch this morning?"

I was happy to come to her aid. Traffic in the Cities was of no interest to me.

"Not much. We walked through the sheds and made sure everything was ready for tomorrow. Wayne showed Lance how he feeds the mink." Lance looked at me with sharp eyes, sure I would relay the feed cart episode. I felt bad for him, having been the frequent victim of Wayne's humiliating sense of humor myself. There was no need to alienate Lance; he was doing a good job of that on his own. My leg was killing me from tramping around in the slush. "It'll be good to be off my feet tomorrow."

Mom held up the platter with the turkey. "Anyone want more? Is everyone getting enough to eat?"

The dish made its way around the table. Lance's eyes relaxed. I asked about his car, and everyone tried to speak at once. Lance looked amused. Mary persisted after the others paused.

"Gwen calls it the Jellybean."

Wayne used his fingers to take a piece of breast meat off the turkey plate. "Some kind of foreign job, isn't it?"

"It's Swedish, a Saab." Lance went on about the advantages of front-wheel drive and low gas mileage. Gwen and Mary said the burned oil smell from the two-stroke engine made them nauseous. Lance said that was the future, small foreign cars would replace big American ones.

A muffled cry came from Mom and Dad's bedroom. Lindsey got up. Gwen turned to Lance. "*That's* the future."

I put my arm around Julia. "That's the future for us too."

Mom's eyes got big.

"Julia, are you expecting?"

"Yes! I'm due in May."

I must have had the stupidest look in the world on my face. Dad looked down at his plate, shook his head and smiled. "Congratulations. I couldn't be happier."

Now that it was in the open, I wasn't sure if it was the biggest mistake of my life, or my greatest achievement.

For most of the meal, Julia had been subdued. It had taken some time for me to persuade her to spend the day with my family rather than hers. Now she brightened with the conversation's shift in her direction. "Gwen, when are you due again?"

"Three weeks to go." She was clearly tired of the question. From the size of her, it appeared she might burst at any moment, but I didn't know anything about pregnancy except how to start one. Gwen put down her silverware. "Julia, are you going to stop working at the hospital?"

"Not right away, I'm going to stop in February. I'll decide later if I'll go back afterward."

Lance straightened up in his chair. "I hope our boys can play together."

Wayne's head was tilting to the left after having had at least three shots. "Will ain't gonna grow up to be no city slicker."

I turned to Lance. "We can teach them how to hunt and fish."

"What if they're girls?" Mary arched her eyebrows.

Gwen tucked her hair behind her ears. "We'll teach them to change the world, and maybe how to run a business if there's spare time."

"Gwen, I hope you don't have to have a C-section like Lindsey did." Mom turned up the side of her mouth.

"Lindsey's too small to handle it the normal way. Although it's good for me." A smile crept across Wayne's face.

"Wayne, I think you've had enough to drink." Dad gave the table a firm pat with his palm.

"I don't think so. You weren't feeding mink at seven this morning after being up most of the night with a screaming kid."

Mom put her hand on Dad's forearm. "Yes, we were. Except it was twenty-five years ago and you were the kid."

"And times weren't as good as they are now, either." The cheer went out of Dad's eyes.

Lance provided a badly needed break when he asked what was for dessert.

"Mom and I made apple, pumpkin, and blueberry pies," Mary said.

"You boys go away while we clear the table. We'll call you when dessert is ready."

"Mom!" Mary pushed away from the table. "We talked about this."

"I need your help clearing the table."

Lance stood up. "Mary, you can go with them. I'll help clear."

"Go with your father," Mom insisted. "Mary and I will take care of this."

We walked into Dad's office at the end of the hall. Dad sat down in the oak desk chair. Lance studied Mary's fishing paintings. I preferred the mounted arrowheads and pipestone pipes on the adjacent wall. They'd been found over the years while digging the foundation for the mink ranch building and adding new sheds.

"Bet there's more of those out there." Wayne said. "Probably could make more money digging the place up and selling the arrowheads than by raising mink. Less work, too."

Lance stepped back from Mary's paintings. "These are quite good. They have amazing texture. The waves look like they're going to roll out of the frame."

I turned to look at the images. "They do capture working on the lake."

"Do you remember what that's like?" Wayne gave Lance a light elbow to the side.

Lance put his face closer to the canvas. "Dad, how did she paint on the boat?"

"She didn't. She came out with us for a week and made drawings. She did the paintings in the high school art studio. Now let's get to it, shall we?"

The ledger book was sitting on the desk. Each year had a tabbed page where the entries began. "I'm glad all of you made it. Between college, the service and accidents, I was starting to wonder if we'd ever do this again." He opened the book to the last page of 1962. "Yesterday, the price of a standard brown pelt was $49.15 in New York. I made a first pass of the income statement using that price."

"If we pelt twenty thousand, that's almost a million in gross revenue." Lance tapped his fingers as if his left hand were an adding machine.

Wayne leaned against the file cabinet next to the desk. "What's this 'we' stuff? I don't remember seeing you work at the ranch last year."

"Knock it off, Wayne." Dad moved his hand down the debit column. "There's wages for you boys, and Jim and Moose, plus property tax on the fishery and the mink farm, electricity, fuel, and all the rest." Dad turned the book toward Lance and pointed at the bottom line.

"Makes the mink smell sweeter, don't it?" Wayne went up on his toes and slowly went back down.

Lance nodded. "Don't get too excited; 91 percent of that three-hundred-thousand-dollar operating profit will go to state and federal taxes."

The grin faded from Wayne's face. "Fuck 'em. The government is trying to put us out of business, and we're giving 'em the money to do it? I say we don't pay in. I could use that money to buy a house."

"Let's hope Kennedy's tax cut passes next year." Dad closed the book. "Maybe we'll be able to keep more than we pay in for once. In the meantime, the sportos and the DNR are still trying to ban pound net licenses. We need to keep the pressure on those legislators. Things are good now, but if we don't do something, we'll lose control of our feed supply."

"Lance, you walk and talk like a politician. You and Dad can go to St. Paul." I didn't know what else to say. The numbers looked good, but I felt in Dad's voice some threat he didn't want to identify. "We could make some campaign contributions."

"Pete, we can't give enough to make a difference." Dad tapped the two-ended pencil he used for ledger entries on the desk. "Lance, what do you suggest?"

"Trawler fishing and the license transfer ban must end. All roads lead to the Capitol."

"I don't trust those bastards in St. Paul." Wayne crossed his arms. "They'll screw us no matter what we do."

"You better get used to dealing with government officials if you want to stay in business," Lance said.

Wayne grabbed Lance by the shoulders and shoved him backward into the wall. "Maybe I didn't go to some East Coast snob factory like you, but I did go to college. I don't need to be schooled."

"You've had too much to drink." Lance started to step around Wayne.

Wayne grabbed Lance's arm. "What's happened to you? You've turned into some kind of dandy, like you're from the Cities. You're a Brennan. You're from here, remember?"

"Believe me, I never forget it." He pushed Wayne's chest with the palms of his hands. "And all those professors in Boston never let me forget it either. To them I was a hick. What *you* call 'God's Country' is called godforsaken in some places."

"So, what are we going to do?" I wanted to stop the pointless arguing. No matter what anyone called Lake of the Woods, I loved it.

"I'll go to St. Paul in January before the legislative session starts." Dad rotated the chair to face us. "I've got to stop trawler fishing. Hold them to the population study results. If I don't, we're done for."

Wayne stroked his beard. "I think we should expand. Make money while we can."

Dad swiveled the desk chair. "Wayne, you read my mind—I've already started a plan to add sheds."

"And how do you expect to finance it?" Lance sat on the couch. "Do you want to put the business into debt?"

I sat down next to Lance. "Who says we need to finance? We take the earnings from this year and use that to cover the expansion."

"What about an emergency fund? What happens if you a need a new engine for the boat or a new tractor?"

"Are you kidding?" Wayne walked to the window and looked out to the street. "I have an emergency right now. I have a kid. I need a decent house. I can't keep living at the ranch."

"Wayne, you can take a loan from retained earnings for a down payment. The rest is going into the expansion."

"Doesn't that mean we'll effectively be owners, if we're getting a share of the profit?"

"It does. I've decided to give each of you a 20 percent share of the business."

"Dad, I don't want a share. I want out." Lance got up off the sofa and took a couple steps toward the door.

I once believed Lance wanted to be involved in the business. After he said he wanted out, I had no more illusions about why he had stayed away for five years.

Wayne stepped away from the window. "Dad, we do all the work, and he gets 20 percent?" He looked ready to smash something. "Why should he get anything?"

"He's one of my sons, and he worked hard to finish his education." Dad gripped the armrests on the chair. His hands turned pale.

"Well, if you insist on giving him something, then why not pay him off?" Wayne stood and glowered in front of Lance. "We don't need his help. We've got by without him for years now."

I agreed. "He's got a job and a house. He doesn't need to be involved. Let him go."

"Equal shares. That's my decision." Dad's gaze passed over each of us.

Lance sighed and slouched against the wall next to the door. "Looks like we're stuck with each other."

"What about Mary?" I said.

"I've put her share in a trust. She'll get it when she turns twenty-one."

Dad's eyes moved over Mary's paintings while he spoke. "I don't want her involved in the business—ever. I want her free of all this."

Lance crossed his arms over his chest. "And why do you want to hold me hostage?"

"Because you're educated and want nothing from the business. If or when a crisis comes, you'll be clear-eyed about what to do."

We looked at each other until I couldn't take it anymore. "Dad, you need to tell Mary now, or she'll never forgive you. Even then she might not."

There was a knock on the door. "Dessert's ready." Mom's footsteps receded in the hall.

"I'll tell her when the time is right." Dad put his hands on the armrests of the office chair. "And I don't want any of you telling her either."

We grumbled our agreement.

Wayne put his hands up. "Are we done? Can we have dessert now?"

We filed out of the office. I was happy to get a stake. The women were waiting for us at the dining room table.

Mary cut the blueberry pie. "So, how did we do last year?"

Lance looked at Dad with sharp eyes. Wayne poured himself a shot and tossed it back.

"Go ahead. Tell her," I said.

Mary sliced the pumpkin pie. "Well?"

"We had a great year." Dad took a piece of pumpkin pie. "Next spring we're going to build more sheds."

Mary stabbed the apple pie. The table vibrated as the blade stuck. "Dad, there's more to it than that."

"We'll talk about it some other time."

Mary jerked the knife out of the pie, and the table. "And I suppose you expect me to help with pelting tomorrow."

"I do," he said. "Your tuition depends on it."

Eight: November 1962

Mary, Lance and Mom perched on metal chairs scattered around the workshop. They shivered, arms and legs held tight against their bodies. It was just after seven o'clock, dark and five below zero outside, maybe fifty inside the ranch building. Mary clutched a plastic cup of coffee. I sat at the workbench that ran along the north wall. We waited for the garage heaters to warm up the space, and for Wayne to come down from the apartment.

Dad walked around checking the equipment. First, he inspected the three skinning machines, which formed a triangle in the middle of the workshop. A fifty-five-gallon drum sat in the center. He moved on to the fleshing beam, a metal frame that held two horizontal cones used to remove fat from pelts.

I arranged the rolling racks used to move pelts to the tumbler along the west wall. The tumbler occupied a room on the opposite end of the building. From the tumbler, pelts were brought back to the shop and mounted on stretching boards. I rifled through the pile of boards to see if any were broken. Once the pelts were mounted and hung on a rack, they were rolled to the walk-in cooler for curing prior to shipment to the tannery.

Wayne arrived half an hour later and looked us over with bloodshot eyes.

"Who's going to kill and who's going to skin?"

The hum of electric motors filled the room.

"Lance? What's it going to be?" Wayne said.

Lance looked as if he had sat down in the wrong classroom. "I'll kill."

"I'll stay here. Make sure everything keeps running," Dad said.

Mom shifted in her seat. "I always skin. You know that."

"I guess I'm fleshing," Mary said.

Wayne pushed his hat back. "You can come with me if you want. There won't be anything to do in here until we get through the first shed."

"I've never killed before." She shook from a chill. "I feel lousy. Maybe some fresh air will help."

"You don't have to kill. You can collect. And Pete, go with them, make sure Sir Lancelot hasn't forgotten how to kill."

"Why me? My leg is throbbing from traipsing around here yesterday."

"You know how to do it right, and we can't wait for Moose and Jim to start next week. We need two killers today. Otherwise, we'll be pelting until after Christmas."

I agreed to nurse Mary and Lance around the yard to get us started. We could finish in three weeks if we made good use of the Thanksgiving weekend.

I reached over to the old radio on the workbench. It had no cover, its forest of tubes visible on a silver base. I turned the left dial with a click and the filaments slowly turned orange.

"How about some Christmas music?"

I rotated the right dial. The orange stick of the tuner moved back and forth in front of an imaginary scale. Ascending and descending levels of static came out of the speaker.

"Let's start with that classical station in Winnipeg. A Strauss waltz or some Mozart would be nice." Dad was not going to give up control of anything easily.

The static ended. Maria Callas' voice burst into the room, hollow and powerful, soaring to a shrill through the middle of *Qual occhio*. Dad's face expanded into a broad smile.

"All right." Wayne looked at Lance and Mary. "Do you have your choppers?"

They held up their thick leather mittens.

"Let's go."

We walked to the shed at the northwest corner of the yard. Chirps and squeaks reverberated among the tin buildings. Tiny puffs of vapor came from the nostrils of the minks, as well as our own noses. The moisture collected in the top of the sheds and formed a layer of ice on the ceiling. Each cage had a tin water tray, the water in the trays frozen solid. Yesterday's feed hung in cone-shaped clumps from the tops of the cages.

"Do you want to use a kill cage or do it by hand?" Wayne said. I was sure Lance would go for the kill cage.

"I've always done it by hand," Lance replied. "You know that."

"Okay, fine. Pete will give you a refresher if you need it. Mary, they'll put them on top of the cages, and you collect them in the cart. You'll collect them faster than they can kill them so you may end up standing around at first."

Lance took the left side of the shed, and I took the right. Killing the first one is the hardest. After the first ten or twenty I would get into the rhythm of it. Lance hesitated, waiting to open the first cage.

"Lance, you can't stare it to death." I reached into the cage. "You have to grab it by the head and the tail." The animal dashed around the cage until I cornered it with my mittens. I closed my hand around its midsection. Despite the heavy leather, the mink's racing heart throbbed against my hands as I lifted it out through the top of the cage. I held it up for Lance to see how I gripped it. Lance's face took on the stillness of the freezing air.

I moved my right hand around the base of the mink's tail and shifted my left hand under its chin. It squirmed in my hands and let out a series of piercing screams which caused the other minks to thrash in their cages. The sound of claws on metal mesh resounded through the shed. After getting the mink under control, I cupped my left hand over its crown, bent down and put my left arm on top of my left thigh. The flailing claws scratched at my choppers and the little body vibrated in my hands. I raised my eyes to meet Lance's, holding the mink steady.

"Lance, you paying attention?"

"Yes—I've done it before, you know." For the first time since he'd been back, I recognized the brother I knew growing up.

"Okay, because I don't want to watch fifty dollars run off into the woods."

I slid my right hand up the mink's body and over its front legs and pressed down as hard as I could. There was a firm snap. The animal stopped moving in my hands. Green excrement trickled onto the right leg of my pants.

I put the dead animal on top of the cage.

Mary stepped forward to view the already stiffening body. "I can't stand here with the cart doing nothing, otherwise I'll freeze. Show me how to use the kill cage."

I took the one hanging at the entrance of the shed and set it on top of the dead mink's cage. Anytime I stopped moving my fingers, the tips burned from the cold.

"Here's how it works. You get the animal out of the cage." I opened the top of the next cage and pulled out the mink as I had before. "Now, use your left hand to guide it." I shoved the animal headfirst into the shoebox-sized device and held its tail with my right hand. Inside, the animal's skull was under a steel plate attached to a twelve-inch handle that stuck out the top. "Keep pressure on its rear end with your right hand and use your left to push down the lever." A metallic crack bounced off the top of the shed. The animal stopped moving. I pulled it out by the tail. "Make sure you push hard and quick. You'll have to do it twice if you don't push hard enough."

Mary's eyes narrowed. "I can do it."

"We'll see. Do the next one."

I opened the top of the next cage. The mink looked up at Mary without moving.

"You can do it," I said. "That's next year's tuition staring back at you."

She grabbed it perfectly and shoved it into the cage. Before the animal could make a sound, the lever came down in a blur. The wind whistled through the ventilators on top of the shed. Lance kicked at the snow. Mary flopped the carcass onto the top of the cage.

"Okay Lance, let's see what you can contribute to my tuition."

He opened the first cage on the left side of the shed. The animal ran in frenzied circles inside. It leaped upward and Lance grabbed it before it escaped, but he had it by the belly and the tail. Its head swung around, trying to bite anything in its way. I grabbed it between my hands and held it while Lance slid his left hand up its body to grab it below the chin. Its teeth pinched my middle finger until Lance slid his hand under mine and cupped its head. He pushed down on the body. Its neck made a slight click. The animal shrieked and thrashed, but its hind legs stopped moving.

"Goddamnit Lance, push like you mean it—now!"

He pushed again and nearly wrapped the animal's body around his left thigh. The dead mink slid to the ground. He stared at it for a moment with his shoulders slumped.

"You're out of practice. I'd lose my edge too if I was away for seven years."

Lance got better by the time we got to the tenth cage. The activity kept us warm. Soon we were moving quickly, a wave of yelping and squealing preceding us.

Mary followed us with the cart, collecting the bodies. She took one off a cage and laid it out on the tray. "How far along was Julia when she told you?"

"Six weeks. She didn't feel well and went to the doctor."

Lance grabbed a mink from a cage and broke its neck on his thigh. He looked at Mary as he set it on top of the cage. "How are you doing?"

"It's good to be outside after being cooped up the last couple days." Mary placed the animal Lance dispatched on top of the others.

"Nothing else going on?" I said.

"Nope."

I didn't believe her. We continued down the row, working steadily, in silence.

At noon, we went into the workshop for lunch. I sat in the first chair I could get to. Wayne distributed the minks from the cart to the skinning machines.

Dad took a mink from a table piled with dead animals. He placed the two front paws in two clamps mounted at the bottom of the skinning machine, with the animal oriented as if it were facing him doing a handstand. He mounted the rear paws in two clamps at the top of the machine. Using a three-inch knife, he cut around the left rear paw, then on a straight line up the back side of the hind leg to the animal's vent, then down the backside of the right leg, and around the right rear paw.

"Everything okay Dad? Any breakdowns?" Wayne said.

"No mechanical ones." He looked at me.

"My leg is killing me."

"Pete, stay in here now that there's animals to pelt. Mary and Lance can keep killing," Dad said.

"I guess we're still on the opera." Wayne pointed to the radio as Caruso sang *Nessun dorma*.

"You can change the station if you want." Dad held up the animal's tail and sliced upward from the base to the end, flipped it out of its skin, and put the raw tail into a clamp between the rear paws. He held onto the tail of the pelt and pushed a pedal. The bracket holding the rear paws moved upward and pulled the carcass from the pelt. Dad unclamped the paws and pulled the pelt over the head. He tossed the carcass into the fifty-gallon drum. It landed with a wet slap against the other carcasses.

The room grew quiet as Mom and Dad stopped skinning. The buzz of the electric motors mixed with the aria on the radio.

We ate peanut butter and brown sugar sandwiches.

Wayne sent Mary and Lance back out to the yard to continue killing. He had me flesh, my least favorite job. Killing is clean, active. Break their neck and move to the next cage. Fleshing had me standing for hours in one place.

I started with the pelts on Dad's skinning table. I took a brown one and put the hind legs over the narrow end of the cone-shaped mandrel, pulling the pelt over it like a sock until the snout was firm against the tip of the cone and the pelt tight against the mandrel. I turned on the blower motor and pushed the scraper blade from the head to the tail in short, firm strokes. After each pass, I rotated the mandrel to scrape a new path. The blower pushed the fat and blood off the scraper blade into a container on the floor. I worked the pelt until white skin appeared. Holding onto the snout, I pulled the pelt off the mandrel and hung it on a rolling rack.

After a couple hours and more than a hundred odd pelts, my forearm was sore. I couldn't put enough pressure on the blade to remove the fat. My knee was turning raw against my prothesis. I sat down to work at a skinning machine.

Later that afternoon, I tossed a carcass toward the barrel. It hit the mound of bodies in the middle and slid over the edge onto the concrete floor.

"You'll never play for the Celtics," Wayne said.

Dad rose from his seat. "Wayne, let's get this barrel out of here."

Wayne picked up the strays from the floor and tucked them in the pile at the top.

Mom went over to the radio. "I think we need some Christmas cheer."

Wayne took a carcass off the top of the barrel and flung it at me. It hit me square on the chest. I picked it up off the floor.

Mom turned toward us from the radio. The melancholy acoustic guitar at the beginning of Peter, Paul and Mary's *A' Soalin'* filled the room.

I walked up to Wayne, holding the body around the hindquarters. Before he could move, I slapped the carcass across his face, then dropped it in the barrel. He cocked his arm to punch me. Dad grabbed him at the elbow. He kicked at me with his right foot. His steel-toed boot smashed into my wooden leg.

I lifted my pant leg. "You put a dent in it."

"Knock that shit off," Dad said. "Now, let's get this barrel out of here."

Dad put his hands on the lip of the barrel and tilted it. Wayne slid the base of the hand truck under the bottom. He wheeled the truck out and we followed him into the cold.

The truck wheels sank in the snow of the main path. We took turns pushing the loaded truck to where we parked "Alice," our orange Allis Chalmers tractor. One full barrel already sat in the front loader.

"If you boys want to sustain this business, you'll have to carry each other. Not fight."

We pushed the barrel off the hand truck and onto the front loader. The bodies in the first barrel had turned gray from the cold. I climbed onto the tractor and started the engine. The flapper on top of the stack bounced with the rhythm of the cylinders.

"Walk out to the junk yard with me," I shouted over the engine. "I'll need help getting these off the loader."

I drove the tractor to the west gate of the yard. In one shed, I saw Lance and Mary at the opposite end, both hunched over with a mink in their hands. The cart was halfway down the shed. Dead animals lay on top of the cages.

"They're making decent progress," Wayne said.

"What?" Dad was looking at a cardinal in a birch tree that stood out against the white landscape.

"Progress. Lance and Mary are going pretty good."

At the gate, Dad struggled to pull the bolt. I tossed him a small hammer we kept in a holster on the back of the tractor seat. He gave the bolt two quick taps, freeing it to slide. I pushed the gate open with the front loader and drove toward a dozen stacks of pallets in the middle of the field.

When we got to the pallets, I stepped off the tractor and let it idle. We pushed over one of the stacks. I dragged the top pallet away from the others toward a spot near the access road.

"Set 'em up here, ya think?" I said.

"That'll be good," Wayne said.

I got back on the tractor and lined up the front edge of the bucket with the edge of the pallet. Again, I got down from the tractor. We got onto the loader and stood on either side of the left-hand barrel. I put my hands on the rim, where I had to push my fingers past the stiffening bodies to get a grip. "On three." As we slid the barrel off the loader onto the pallet, the snow underneath crunched. Dad grimaced when he let go of the barrel.

I stepped over to the other drum. "Your back okay?"

"It's good enough." Dad bent forward at his waist, then back.

We repeated the process with the other barrel. The cardinal landed briefly on the tractor seat. Dad watched it flutter off to a pine tree.

"Wayne, did you schedule the rendering truck?"

"I did." He rolled two empty barrels onto the front loader. "It's going to come every Friday."

"Good. I'd hate to think some poor dog in the Cities might have to go without its dinner." He rested his hands on the rim of the second barrel as if he had finished a fifty-yard dash.

"Do you want to drive the tractor back?" I said.

"No, I'll walk. I want to watch the birds."

In the workshop, Mel Torme crooning *The Christmas Song* drifted from the radio. Pelts from the tumbler were on racks parked around the room. Pine stretching boards, seasoned from yellow to brown by pelts over the years, lay stacked on the workbench.

It was dark outside when the last rack went to the tumbler. After finishing in the yard, Lance and Mary started running the other two fleshers. Dad and I started in on stretching. We stood around a stainless-steel table, taking a pelt from a rack, pulling it over a board, and hanging it on another rack. When Lance and Mary finished fleshing, they joined us.

Lance's shoulders tilted forward from spending the afternoon bent over killing. Wayne started in on him right away. "How does it feel to do real work?"

"Finding ways to feed more people *is* real work. Although it doesn't involve as much blood and shit as dealing with you."

"He finished college, which is more than you can say." I drew a pelt over a board. Wayne probably didn't expect me to stand up for Lance, so he came after me.

"St. Peter speaks. We haven't heard from you for a while."

"I'm a fisherman, not a saint."

"God help us. Our rock and our foundation stands on one leg."

"Less talk and more work." Mary cracked a sapphire hide like a whip. "My tuition is due after Christmas, and I want to get out of here at a decent hour."

Wayne hung up a stretched pelt. "You'd make a good boss."

"Fuck you, Wayne." Mary wonked him on the back with a stretching board.

"Mary!" Mom's face lit up in exasperation as she pushed a rack from the tumbling room.

"As if Dad would allow me to do anything other than shit work."

"C'mon, Mary." Dad hung a stretched pelt.

"Why wouldn't you let me see the ledger? I don't count? Is that it?" She walked past Dad, hung the board on a rack, and returned to the table. "Well? Do I?"

Dad stammered. "I expect after college you'll get married and stay in the Cities or move to some other place."

Mary picked a stretching board off the pile. "So what? Lance did."

"He's the oldest." Dad reached for the ancient defense. "I'll let you know the plan in good time."

She dropped the board and walked toward the door. "I'm done with this." She slammed the door behind her.

"Mary's right." I pointed a board at Wayne. "She should have been in Dad's office with us yesterday."

"Pete, don't be a sissy." Wayne grabbed the stretching board at the opposite end and pulled it out of my hand. He prodded me with it like a sword.

"That's enough you two," Dad said. "Let's finish up and get out of here. Start fresh tomorrow."

I exhaled and stretched my back. We worked for another hour to finish stretching the day's pelts. I didn't get home until 8:30 that night. Julia was working a night shift at the hospital. The house moaned with the cold.

Day one of pelting was over. Three weeks to go.

Nine: June 1966

The man sat forty feet away on the end of the dock, casting a line into the river. The whine from the reel floated in the June air. He wore patched jeans and a plaid shirt with the store folds still visible. A canvas daypack sat in a heap next to him.

Jim climbed down the seven-foot ladder to the boat. Moose followed, then Dad. I handed down our lunch boxes.

A flash caught my eye. The spinner on the man's line swooped out over the water. The lure splashed into the river. He turned to face me. There wasn't any stubble on his cheeks or chin. His left hand went up in a tentative wave. I waved back. He turned away to reel in the lure.

Jim, Moose and Dad stood near the gunwale as I went down the ladder. Jim helped me off the ladder onto the deck.

"You ever see him before?" Jim said.

"No," I said.

The others shook their heads.

Jim went to the bow and Moose to the stern to release the mooring lines. Dad stood next to me in the pilothouse while I started the engine. He told me he wanted to lift the nets off Elm Point. After a warm, calm night, he expected we'd have a big catch.

Elm Point is a small, tree-covered peninsula that sticks out of the neck of Buffalo Point. Due to an incorrect map used during the Treaty of Paris negotiations at the end of the Revolutionary War, the western border between the United States and Great Britain's North American territories was set as the northwest corner of Lake of the Woods, south to the 49th parallel, and west to the Pacific Ocean. Ben Franklin and the English negotiators didn't know the 49th parallel sliced off Elm Point from Buffalo Point. This put the buffalo's head in Canada and Elm Point in the United States, creating a half-mile-long, unpatrolled frontier.

I slowed the engine when the point came into view. A dense tangle of tamarack, birch and spruce trees formed a green wall behind the black and beige rocks of the shoreline. Cardinals, goldfinches and orioles hopped among the tree branches.

Jim and Moose secured the mooring lines, and we began to lift the pound into the boat. Jim thanked the fish. Each swell compressed the pad between my stump and my leg, sending a throbbing sensation up my back.

"You ready for the wedding?" Moose said.

"I think so." I pulled a bundle of black netting over the side. "I'm still trying to believe it's happening."

"Between you, me and the fish, I'm not thrilled," Dad said. "But they have to do it under the circumstances. Now we're going to be related to those people. We can't ignore them."

"Dad, it could be worse. She could be marrying some French artist instead of Eddie Worland."

"I wish she *were* going to France, but don't tell your mother I said that. Sure, it'll be nice to have her in town. I thought she would marry some artist and move to Paris or New York. I never thought the thing with Eddie would last."

"The Worlands have money. She can do all the painting she wants."

"It's not the same. She'd get exposed to things she'd never see around here."

"There's things here she'd never see in those places."

"Look at this day." Jim raised his arms. "Sun, quiet and clean air. New York and Paris are noise, people and shit. There's none of that out here. On the water is the best place to be."

"I'll second that," I said. A seagull's cry spread out over the water, rolled up the trees on shore, and echoed back to us.

"How is it that Eddie escaped the draft?" Moose stopped lifting with a bunch of net at his waist. "I hear they're sending more guys to Vietnam every day."

"Cal is on the draft board." Dad pulled a bundle of net over the gunwale. "He has five boys—and not one served. In fact, that son of a bitch refused to give Lance an education deferment back in fifty-six. Here we are ten years later, and his boys got deferments for everything from eyesight to foot fungus. I'm just glad my boys finished their service before this nonsense in Vietnam got started."

"Arthur, your sons became warriors," Jim said. "You should be proud. His boys did nothing to earn their privilege. Calvin Worland may have made himself rich, but he has no honor."

I didn't feel honor in the service. I was bored, lost, tired and scared. I worried about letting my outfit down. Every night I thought about getting back to the lake. I was a fisherman, not a warrior. I didn't feel honor after I got home, either.

The guy was still at the end of the dock when we returned to the fishery. Three walleyes hung on a stringer tied to the dock piling. I rolled a load of fish boxes from the dock to the scale inside the fishery. On my way back for the next load, he smiled and waved at me. I nodded. The buzz of his reel spread over the river. The lure plopped into the water.

He was there again the next morning, in the same clothes, next to the bag, casting. Low clouds strained the orange sunlight into beams. He turned toward us when we clomped onto the dock, a brown shadow surrounding his mouth and chin. He raised his left arm in a wave—several blades of grass hung off his sleeve. The skin around his eyes was dark and puffy. I heard the others descend the ladder to the deck. I waved back, handed the lunch boxes to Jim, and climbed down.

"Buffalo Point?"

Dad nodded. "The wind will be in our faces all day."

We had nearly finished lifting the second net when Dad groaned and slipped backward. He fell into a seated position against some fish boxes and clutched the right side of his groin.

"It's that goddamn hernia."

I crouched down next to him. "You've managed before. Can you stand up?"

"I think it really popped this time."

Jim put his hands on Dad's shoulders. "Sit still." He felt around Dad's groin. Dad shuddered under the pressure. "It's pushed through all right." Jim guided Dad's hand. "Feel that bulge?"

Dad nodded.

"You're done working for a while."

"You guys are starting to break down." Moose leaned against the pilothouse.

"What the hell is that supposed to mean?" I slapped him in the chest.

"Your leg, and now this."

"Get the goddamn dipper ready so we can finish." Dad tried to stand up.

"Dad, you're done. We'll dip the pound, reset the net and head in."

Jim and I lifted him off the deck. He felt lighter than I expected. His eyes narrowed in pain. His face turned red, accentuating the deep lines around his eyes and mouth. We sat him down on the bench at the back of the pilothouse, making sure he didn't bump his head on the rifle. In a moment, he'd diminished from the powerful father I grew up with to an old man I didn't recognize.

At the fishery, we unloaded Dad first. There was a winch crane on the dock made from a piling pole with a cast-iron pulley at the end. We used the crane to lift the fish boxes out of the boat two at a time and onto a dolly. Moose climbed up the ladder to operate the crane, while Jim and I got Dad to stand in an empty fish box. We secured the winch rope around the four handles. Dad put on a pair of leather gloves and held onto the rope with his left hand.

"I think you should use both hands," I said.

He held up his right hand, spinning his index finger—the signal to hoist. Moose engaged the winch and Dad grabbed the rope with his right hand.

Jim patted him between the shoulders. "Have a nice flight."

The box lifted off the deck. Jim and I steadied the bottom of the box. The skin around Dad's jaw puffed out as he looked down at us. We pushed the box toward the dock as it rose. A pair of hands reached out and guided the box onto the dock.

"That's quite a catch," said an unfamiliar voice.

"Ha ha." Dad stepped out of the box with help from Moose.

I climbed up the ladder. It was him—the casting fisherman.

"Thanks for that," I said.

He nodded at me and walked back to the end of the dock.

"Moose, can you take Dad home? Jim and I will unload."

The sun was high in the west. Dad leaned against Moose as they walked toward the building. They produced a single shadow, Moose's greater stature eclipsing Dad. I wondered if it was their last day fishing.

After we finished unloading, I walked back to the end of the dock. The man watched the water flow past with a blank expression.

"What brings you around here?" I said.

"I just finished college. I'm figuring out what to do next."

"What did you study?"

"History."

"Not many jobs in that."

"I learned what people did with their lives, but I don't know what to do with mine. I thought of becoming a lawyer or a teacher when I started college. Now I'm not sure."

"Pete Brennan." I extended my hand. "Fishing's a good life, but a hard one."

He shook with a firm grip, one that indicated he'd been around men who worked outside, rather than the crunching grip of someone trying to prove their strength.

"Roger Fixx. That's with two x's. My dad's a builder in Mankato. I grew up around job sites. That's a hard life too."

"You need work to get by while you figure it out? They're looking for people at Worland's."

"I don't want to work in a factory. I spent the last four years in dark libraries and small dorm rooms. Space is what I need."

"We could use another guy on the boat. My dad went down with a hernia today."

"Really? I sure could use some pocket money."

"Let me talk it over with the other guys."

After supper, I told Julia I was going to the Number Two. She crossed her arms over her chest, her right hip stuck out like an accusing finger.

"You try spending the day dealing with a three-year-old and an eight-month-old. I know you work hard, but I need to get out or I'm going to lose my sanity."

"I won't be long. We need to figure out if we want to take another guy on the boat, since Dad can't work. I'll be back in time to put Jay and Rob to bed."

Jim, Wayne and Moose were sitting at a table opposite the bar. Vern said hello as I walked in. People recovering from a day in the Worland factory sat at the bar in various slouches, their clothes sprinkled with sawdust. Some turned and waved, others stared at their reflections in the mirror behind the bar.

"You know that guy who was at the fishery today?"

Jim and Moose nodded. Wayne looked puzzled. I told him what had happened the last two days.

"What makes you think this guy can work?" Wayne peered over a row of brown bottles.

"He's hungry. I think he's sleeping outside in the park. Probably needs some money."

"Probably hitchhiked to get here, too. Maybe one of the Worland truck drivers picked him up." Jim rotated the glass in front of him with his fingers.

"What makes you say that?" Moose struck a match and lit a roll-your-own.

"I've heard about guys coming up here, trying to get to Canada."

"I don't care where he's trying to go. We need another man. I told him we'd talk it over tonight and that he could stay upstairs at the fishery in the office. Dad never uses it anyway."

"Why'd you do that?" Wayne drank from the bottle at the end of the row. "The guy could be a murderer, a bank robber, or who knows what. We—no, you—could be harboring a fugitive. What if he burns the place down getting high?"

"You haven't seen him. He's a college kid from Mankato. Roger Fixx is his name. He'll work for a while, get some callouses on his hands, and go back home to be a lawyer or a teacher like he told me. In the meantime, Dad gets his surgery and he's ready to go for pelting."

"Pete, Dad isn't going to want a stranger living upstairs in the fishery."

"I'm running the fishing business while Dad's out, and I think we should give the guy a chance. I'll deal with Dad. How about if we take him out tomorrow and see how it goes?"

"I don't mind," Moose blew a cloud of white smoke over us. "I can handle him if he gets out of line."

Wayne took the last swallow from his beer. "All right, just make sure he doesn't lose any limbs, okay?"

The next morning, I expected to find Roger asleep in the office. He spun around in the desk chair when I opened the door. A ball of white stuffing floated out from the chair's padding and drifted to the dust-covered floor.

"Still want to go?" I said.

"You betcha." His voice had the flatness of someone from south of the Cities.

"The other guys will be here in about fifteen minutes. You'll need to pick out some oilers downstairs."

"Is the weather going to change? It looks good right now."

"There's a lot of flopping fish and splashing. You have any other clothes?"

"I have some of my dad's old army fatigues."

"Wear those. Whatever you have on will get damp and stink like fish."

"Can I do laundry somewhere? I'll need them later."

"There's a washer and dryer in City Park next to the toilets. There's a shower there too. You'll want to use it after you're done, at least if you want anyone to talk to you."

I went down the stairs to the big open room with the scale, loading platform and ice crusher, while Roger changed clothes. When he came down, I told him to look for oilers under the stairs. Yellow and green foul-weather gear hung on brass hooks screwed into the bare joists. Below them stood a line of tall rubber boots.

"Are they arranged by size?"

"This isn't Dayton's, man, grab what looks like might fit and try it on."

He took a pair of pants off a hook.

"Don't stuff the pant legs into your boots," I said. "If you go into the drink, your pants will fill up and you'll sink like a stone."

Jim and Moose came into the room as Roger was trying on jackets. I introduced them and said we were going to the nets off Springsteel Island.

Roger smiled. "I heard that island has a nice resort."

Jim shook Roger's hand. "It does, but we're not going there for a vacation."

I had Roger stand between Moose and me on the first net. The red cabins on the south shore of the island stood out from the green foliage.

Moose asked him if he knew any knots. He said he had learned a few in the Boy Scouts, although he hadn't tied one to hold anything. His dad's building sites always employed riggers. Jim said he ought to practice tying knots if he expected to work on a boat for long.

Once the pound had been lifted, I went to the dipper controls. The surface of the pound boiled with tullibees. I told Roger to stand out of the way. Moose guided the scoop over four fish boxes in the stern. I grabbed the other side with my right hand while keeping my left on the winch control. Moose pulled the cord at the bottom. Two hundred pounds of twisting fish poured out into the pine boxes and onto the deck.

"Roger, watch your step. You'll go down in a hurry if your foot lands on a fish." I pointed forward. "Now get two boxes from the bow and put them on top of the four we just filled."

Moose grabbed two boxes and arranged them next to the ones Roger put down. We continued the routine until the pound was empty and the four-box arrangement was six boxes high.

We ate lunch before we moved on to the second net. We sat in the bow on empty fish boxes with our food on our laps, handing Roger bits of sandwich, chips and cookies we could spare. Jim offered him a cigarette, which he declined. The wind picked up while we ate. Roger didn't show any signs of seasickness. He moved confidently around the boat.

As we put our lunch boxes away, Anders Bergstrom's trawler rumbled around the Northeast side of the island. Anders tooted the boat's whistle. Moose held up his left hand and extended his middle finger. Anders responded with two short toots. On the trawler's stern, three men were deploying the trawl bag.

At the second net, the choppy sound of a speed boat bucking the waves rolled over us. We pulled the pound in twice as fast as usual. I had gotten used to a slower pace in the last couple years as Dad's strength waned. At the pace we were going, we'd have no trouble getting all three Springsteel Island nets lifted by mid-afternoon.

I asked Roger if he wanted to try handling the dipper scoop. He agreed and moved to the center of the starboard side. Jim got the dipper down and Roger took hold of the scoop. As he let go, the crack of a rifle shot ripped the air. I saw a puff hanging over the water near a red and white speed boat. A moment later the tinging from the bullet's impact on the hull of Anders's trawler reached us. Roger scrambled around the fish boxes and hid on the opposite side of the pilothouse. A second crack sounded a moment later, followed by the delayed tinging sound.

"Moose, get the binoculars and see if you can get that boat's number."

The increasing whine of the speedboat's motor reached us out of sync with the image of it plowing through the waves. The driver headed northeast, away from the trawler—and us. He knew which direction to go to get away from the Coast Guard.

"Too far away." Moose had the binoculars over his eyes. "Should I get Anders on the radio?"

"Yeah, see if they're all right."

"How about if we get this first scoop on board so we're not sitting here with our pants down?" Jim said.

"Roger, get your shit together and grab that scoop." Roger's eyes were wide, as if I had asked him to jump off a building. "They're not interested in us. They're anglers who want to stop that trawler from taking all the fish."

"You sure?"

"Positive. They're probably heading toward the islands in Canada, where they can lay low. In a couple days they'll cruise back to Worland or Baudette unnoticed, like any other fishing party."

"Don't worry." Jim had a big smile on his face. "You'll get used to gunfire after you've been in the service. They train you to run toward it instead of away from it."

Moose came out of the pilothouse. "Anders says they're okay. Just shaken up a little. He thinks he knows who it was."

"My guess is sportos from the Cities."

We finished bailing the pound, filling twelve more fish boxes. The catch was half the size of the first. While I didn't agree with the sportos' method, I wanted the same outcome they did.

A week after Roger started working with us, I paid him seventy-five dollars cash. He put it in a rubber tobacco pouch. I asked him if he had figured out what he wanted to do.

"I'm getting closer. I like the way you guys live."

"You don't know the half of it. Winter is much colder here than in Mankato. We spend the winter mending nets. I grew up with it, but it's not a life most people would want."

"Where are we going today?"

"Elm Point."

We'd finished lifting the first net when Roger said he needed to take a leak. He went to the port side while Moose, Jim and I got the dipper ready to bail the net.

"You sure you're pointing the right direction?" Jim said. Moose, Jim and I laughed.

That's when we heard the splash.

Jim grabbed the life ring hung on the back of the pilothouse. Roger flailed away in the water, attempting a crawl stroke. The yellow oiler jacket billowed around his chest. Jim flung the ring. It slapped into the water behind Roger's churning arms.

He ignored it.

I went to the front of the pilothouse, but Jim got there first. He pulled the rifle from its rack over the bench.

"Don't," I said.

Jim grabbed the ammunition box.

"Shoot the son of a bitch!" Moose pumped his arm toward Roger.

"Jim, they'll throw away the key, no matter what you did in the service."

"He's getting away." Moose leaned against a stack of fish boxes. "It's just us and him. Bodies wash up all the time around here."

Roger stopped swimming and started to tread water. He struggled to pull off the oiler jacket.

I said, "Leave him to the Border Patrol or the Mounties."

Jim tore open the ammunition box. Cartridges spilled out on the bench and rolled onto the deck.

"Goddamnit!" He tossed the rifle onto the bench.

We lined up on the port side. Roger got the jacket off and dangled from the second to last piling. He faced a quarter-mile swim to the shore. I grabbed the gunwale. "It'll be a hard swim in those wet clothes."

Jim kicked the side of the pilothouse. "Fuck." He glared at me. "Listen, I wouldn't wish the experience I had in the Pacific on anyone, and I hear 'Nam is the same or worse, but that kid has a duty."

"I say we leave him there," Moose slapped the gunwale. "Let him swim for it if he wants to get away so bad. Maybe he dies here instead of in the jungle."

Roger slung himself along the lead to the last piling while we argued. His wet shirt clung to his arms. The life ring rose and twisted on the swells. Moose pulled in the lifeline until the ring bounced on the hull. He hauled it over the side and slammed it onto the fish-covered deck.

Roger swam slowly toward the shore, a black spot in the water.

"You swim for it, motherfucker," Moose yelled. "And don't come back!"

"The bears are gonna have a delicacy tonight," Jim shouted. "Go! Go! Go!"

I started to yell too. "Swim! Pull! You can make it!"

We yelled at him until he crawled up on the shore. I got the binoculars from the pilothouse and found him splayed over the rocks with a smile on his face. I still don't know if it was the stupidest or the bravest thing I ever saw.

He didn't look back.

Ten: August 1966

The photographer arranged the wedding party in a semicircle. To Eddie's left were three of his brothers and Lance, in gray suits with silver ties, the sun reflecting off the tops of their shoes. To Mary's right were Camilla, Julia, Lindsey, and Gwen, in royal blue dresses. Mom, Dad and I stood off to the side in the shadow of the church. Mom and Dad had their arms around each other, a sight I'd seen only a few times. Maple leaves fluttered in the light wind.

Calvin Worland put his hand on Dad's shoulder. "Bring back any memories?"

"No, actually. Ginny and I eloped. Our families were against the marriage."

"Ginny, you look magnificent." Laura Worland grinned. "Those hair and makeup people from the Cities are miracle workers, aren't they?"

"They are indeed. You've never looked better," Mom responded.

The Worlands had flown in a hair and makeup artist on their plane to prepare all the women for the big day. Mom had begrudgingly subjected herself to the artist's hand, telling me earlier that morning that her hair felt like a hat from all the hair spray.

The photographer dismissed the men and lined up the women for a bridal party photo. Camilla, Mary's maid of honor, laughed and lifted the hem of her skirt, revealing black high cut basketball shoes while she took her place to Mary's right.

Laura scrunched her face. "Where did Mary find that one?"

"St. Kate's. She's a MacLaughlin." Mom deadpanned.

"You mean a Global Grain MacLaughlin?"

"Yes. I thought you and Cal knew all the society people in the Cities."

We watched the photographer arrange and rearrange the young women in front of some pine trees. Then there were shots of each bridesmaid. Julia looked to be enjoying herself, having some time away from our two boys, who were corralled with all the other kids in the church basement. She spun around pretending to be a movie star, and the photographer played along. Gwen was businesslike for her turn, doing as the photographer asked and showing relief when she was done. Lindsey looked anemic, the result of caring for three children under five. Camilla refused to do the standard poses, frustrating the photographer. Mary and Camilla posed together, with Mary gamely showing her garter and Camilla morphing into a graceful *passé*, looking beyond the camera and accentuating her black, rubber-soled shoes.

The photographer dismissed Mary and Camilla. "Parents? Are we ready?"

Cal took out a flask from inside his jacket. "Anyone need reinforcement?" He unscrewed the cap and held out the container.

"No thanks," I said. Julia had given me firm instructions before we left the house.

Dad took the flask. "*Sláinte*, Cal." He raised it to his mouth. "This is wedding number four for you as well, isn't it?"

"It is." A grin spread across Cal's face. "Be glad she isn't showing for the pictures."

"That scotch, Cal?" Dad handed the flask to Laura.

"Yes."

Laura swallowed as if washing down aspirin. "What is *sláinte*?"

"It's a toast to your health," Dad said. "Cal, you should have Irish whiskey in your flask, not scotch."

"Do you want to refight the Battle of the Boyne right here?" Cal raised his fists.

"Those Irish traditions are so cute." Laura handed the flask back to Cal.

"On second thought, I think I'll have a nip," I said. Cal passed the flask to me.

The photographer had one hand resting on top of the tripod-mounted camera. "Any time you folks are ready."

I held out the flask to Cal.

"You keep it. We'll have something to toast later."

Mary and Eddie each had their own minister for the ceremony. Father Shannon, our pastor at St. Patrick's, and Reverend Shaw, the Worland's minister at St. Edward's, stood uncomfortably in front of the altar. Reverend Shaw, in red and white vestments, shifted his feet, looking around as if he couldn't find his car in a parking lot, while Father Shannon, in green and gold, moved the Bible in his hands back and forth so much that I thought he might take out two more and start juggling them. After that, I imagined them with heavily painted clown faces juggling Bibles behind the communion rail.

I turned around to find out the cause of an erupting ruckus behind me. Wayne held Jay and Will's locked right hands, their elbows balanced on the back of the pew between them, as they prepared to arm-wrestle. Percival, Lance's son, took a hymnal from the seat back holder. He started to tap my leg with it, fascinated by the hollow sound.

"Pete, get those boys to behave," Mom said from the row ahead of me.

"Mom, the next hour is going to be boring for them." I grabbed the hymnal from Percival's hand. "If they can have a little fun now, maybe they'll be good later on."

Before I could say anything more, Wayne whispered, "Three. Two. One." Will held his right elbow with his left hand. Jay stood on the seat and used his legs to push against Will's arm. In a quick thrust, Will pounded Jay's hand onto the wooden seat back.

"Ow!" Jay's outburst rode on top of the organ music. "You didn't have to do it so hard!"

Wayne let out a laugh, then caught himself. He pushed Will back on the seat next to him. Jay withdrew and sat down next to me. Percival laughed and poked Jay. "You're a loser." After they started pushing each other, I got up and sat between them.

Across the aisle, Cal and Laura whispered to each other. Cal looked at me, pointed to the lump in my breast pocket, and tilted his head to the side with a questioning look. I wanted to take another belt right there. The wedding march started, and Dad joined Mom in the front pew after delivering Mary to Eddie Worland. The ceremony proceeded as planned—in duplicate—the couple exchanging vows twice to make their marriage legitimate in their separate churches.

The reception was in City Park. Getting out of the church into the fresh air cleared my head. In the center of the park was a square gazebo, painted white with green trim, where the bar and food were set up. White tablecloths covered rectangular folding tables arranged in a square. A clear vase with cattails, black-eyed susans and coneflowers anchored the tablecloths. The gazebo and the lake served as a backdrop to the head table. Buffalo Point, green and shimmering, floated on top of the dark blue horizon.

Eddie and Mary took their places at the head table. Eddie talked over his right shoulder to one of his brothers, their shadows creating a long dark patch on the grass. Camilla set a plate in front of Mary. They caught me looking at them and waved and smiled. Julia came over to where I was sitting with Jay and Robert.

"Maybe we should have a soiree like this for ourselves, since we didn't get one."

"Why? Haven't the last four years been one long party?"

"They have." Julia kissed me. The light breeze had tousled her hair. I used my fingers to smooth it back into place and kissed her on the mouth.

Lance put a plate in front of me. "Mom did a hell of a job putting this together."

"She didn't do it alone." I pointed to the chairs reserved for Calvin and Laura.

"I bet she wishes she'd had all boys." Lance laughed. "Where *are* the Worlands?"

"Probably talking about mullions or sashes to some poor soul."

"What was going on with Percival and Jay?" Dad's annoyance flashed out of nowhere like a beacon.

"I think Pete and Wayne like to see the kids run wild," Mom said.

"Those two are a volatile mixture," Lance said. "Yesterday I caught them trying to open the safe in Dad's office."

"They're okay," Dad said. "Boys need to get in trouble once in a while; that's how they learn the ways of the world."

Calvin and Laura appeared as if they had been conjured. Laura stood next to her chair looking around, waiting. Dad stood and pulled out the chair for her while Cal sat down.

"Well, they went through with it. Welcome to the Worland family."

"Welcome to the Brennan family."

Cal's expression transformed into concern, like he'd boarded a bus with unpleasant looking passengers. Bob Worland and Camilla arrived with plates for Cal and Laura.

"Camilla, those are lovely shoes you're wearing." Laura never missed an opportunity.

"Mrs. Worland, I'd be happy if I never wore heels or a dress again."

"You must be one of those women's libbers," Cal said.

"Watch out Mr. Worland, Mary has it in spades too. She doesn't show it. Someday she's going to come out of her shell."

"I like my shell," Mom said. "It protects me."

"What in the world are you people talking about?" Laura said.

"Things are changing, aren't they Bobby." Camilla tugged on Bob's arm. He shrugged and looked at his father.

"Arthur, how's the fishing?" Cal waved off Bob and Camilla with a genial flourish.

"It's okay." The furrows over his nose gave away his irritation with Cal's barbed graciousness. "It would be better if you hadn't supported the trawler bill."

"I have to protect my own interests." Cal's amiable disposition evaporated. "The state threatened to take away my logging permits in this grand mess."

"But you were content to let them take away my source of mink feed."

Laura tried gamely to intervene. "Let's not talk about business. Okay?"

Cal put his left hand on top of her right in a firm grip without looking away from Dad. She tried to pull her hand out. He clamped it down on the table.

"You've got to put on your own life jacket before trying to save others." Cal flung off Laura's hand as if it had suddenly become hot. "You know Arthur, I heard you had a hired man go over the side a few weeks ago."

"Not everyone can have their father on the draft board, Cal." Dad sipped his water. "Anyway, I'm going out next week for the first time since my surgery. We'll be back to business as usual soon."

"You're a smart man, Arthur, an educated man." Cal snapped his napkin into place. "You could do good work for us without working so hard or hurting yourself."

"I like my independence. I did more for you than I should have when I showed you how to bend wood."

"Fishing and mink farming aren't going to last forever." Cal had misplaced his usually subtle ruthlessness. "Although I have some information about that which may interest you."

"Is that why I'm still carrying around your flask?" I said.

"I've seen the fish population study. It shows a measurable decline. According to what I hear at the Capitol, the trawler license will not be renewed. And they won't bother me anymore about logging permits. It appears you'll receive a stay of execution. What is that word you toasted with earlier?"

"*Sláinte.*" I handed him the flask. "I'd rather not toast if you don't mind."

"I don't. All of you will end up working for me someday sooner or later. Looks like it will be later, for now."

"You'll never get Lance," Mom said. "He's escaped already."

"The MacLaughlins got him," Cal chuckled.

Jay ran past, with Percival chasing him. Percival's white shirt had a red stain on the chest and Jay's pants were torn on one knee. They circled an old elm. Jay chose the wrong direction, and they collided. I collected Jay in my arms and sat the stunned four-year-old on my lap.

"Neither you nor the MacLaughlins are getting this one."

Part II: Jay

Eleven: July 1973

In one of my earliest memories, Dad picks me up off the grass and sets me on his lap. I'd knocked myself silly colliding with Percival under a big tree in City Park at Aunt Mary's wedding. I struggle to get comfortable with the straps and buckles of his artificial leg poking my rear end. He won't let me go while talking to Grandpa Brennan and Calvin Worland.

Every time after that, when Uncle Lance came to Worland, Percival and I would get thrown together to keep ourselves busy—and out of trouble.

It didn't work. The trouble started on a hot July afternoon. We'd watched fireworks the night before with our parents, from the town beach. Percival got sent over to our house after putting his hand through a glass door at Grandpa Brennan's. He'd been chasing my cousin Aoife, his sister, around the yard after she'd dropped his transistor radio—and the plug-in earphone—in the toilet.

I waited for him on the front steps with my baseball glove. Mom had warned me that he was coming, and that Lance had instructed him to play catch. He waved when he came into the yard. His black hair hung over his face, like his mother's.

"You got in trou-ble," I sang in an "I'm-glad-I'm-not-you" tenor.

"Aoife closed the door too fast. It wasn't my fault." He said she deserved to be hit. Now he wouldn't be able to listen to baseball games because she's wrecked his radio. He held up his glove. "Wanna play catch?"

"Okay."

I walked off the stoop and stood in the ankle-high grass, trying to put a left-hand glove on my right hand.

"Do you play in Little League?" he asked.

"No."

"You should. My favorite player is Rod Carew. Who's yours?"

I got the glove on my left hand. "We don't have Little League."

He rolled the ball the forty feet between us.

"Throw it back."

I pushed it into my palm, not knowing how to hold it. When I threw it, the ball flew at a sharp angle onto the ground and rolled to a stop twenty feet away. He walked to the ball and picked it up, holding it so I could see his fingers across the seams. I took the ball from him and held it as he showed me. I tossed it in a high arc. He caught the ball in front of his chest. "Good one. Here it comes."

I held my glove up parallel to the ground, as if it were a saucepan. The ball hit the heel of the glove and plopped to the ground. He told me to hold the glove palm out, as if I wanted to block the sun from my eyes. I flung the ball as hard as I could, and by some miracle it flew in a straight line. He caught it and quickly fired it back. I locked my elbow, waving the glove as a shield. The ball sailed past me into the neighbor's garden, landing in a tangle of tomato and zucchini plants.

"I don't want to do this anymore."

"One more and we'll quit."

I walked into the garden and knelt in the dirt, threading my arm through the vines. This time I rolled the ball back. Percival fielded it and threw it as hard as he could at my chest. In a panic, I held the glove palm-up. The ball bounced off the heel and hit me in the lower lip. Blood dribbled onto my chin. I threw the glove down and ran to the house. "I hate playing catch!"

Mom met me at the door. "What happened?"

"Percy hit me with the ball."

"I did not! You don't know how to catch."

"Let's get some ice on that lip. Percival, I think you should go back to Grandpa and Grandma's now."

Mom closed the door. Through the window, I saw Percival pick up the ball and throw it down the street, where it dented the roof of a gray Buick and rolled out of sight.

The day after Percival smashed the window, Dad dragged me to the mink ranch. Dad and Grandpa talked over Alice, going back and forth about what might be wrong with it. Dad spent most of his time with Grandpa talking about broken propellers, misfiring engines and faulty wiring over drinks that smelled like kitchen cleaner or the broken machinery itself. I sat in the metal seat watching them fiddle with spark plug cables and a socket wrench. Dad told me to get down and stay out of their way.

I wandered off to a mink shed. The minks raced around their cages. If I stopped in front of a cage, the animal would look up, its head bobbing up and down. At the far end of the shed, Uncle Wayne entered on the feed cart, the sputtering of the engine bouncing its way toward me. He stopped at each cage, deposited a blob of food on top, and rolled forward to the next.

"What's happening, boy?"

He wore a Red Man tobacco hat, his cheek bulged with snus, and a smile flashed behind his red beard.

"Not much." I rested my right hand on top of a cage.

"Don't stick your fingers in them cages if you don't want to lose 'em." He spit in the dirt next to the front wheel.

"When am I going to get the Puffer Kite you promised me?"

"Next time I'm in the Cities."

"You never go to the Cities."

"I will if Lance invites me."

I told him we saw a black bear digging in a trash can at a wayside rest the last time I went to the Cities.

"You know, me and your dad ran into a bear last year while we were deer hunting."

"You did not."

"Did too. We were bowhunting, minding our own business, and this bear walks out from behind a tamarack. I gave my bow to your dad and shot the bear with my pistol. He was so close, I pret' near was able to pet him, and then he ran off."

I stared at him, trying to figure out if he was telling the truth. A low rumble came from the opposite end of the shed.

"Sounds like they got the tractor running." He leaned down toward me, cupping his hand around his mouth. "Your dad can fix anything. Fishing is a waste of his talent."

"I hand him tools while he works on the car."

"That's good, you might learn something. Now go see how they're doing so I can finish this shed."

I ran down the aisle and out into the sunshine on the main path. Near the ranch building, Dad was sitting in the seat of the idling tractor. Grandpa was looking up at him, pointing at the sky. Dad pushed a lever forward, and the front loader moved off the ground. He smiled and waved for me to come over.

Grandpa pointed to the tractor step and extended his hand. Dad pulled me up between himself and the fender. We drove around the yard next to the electric fence.

"Uncle Wayne said fishing is a waste of your talent."

"Driving a feed cart is a waste of his talent. You know, he and Grandpa built all these sheds and the main building themselves."

The tractor bounced in a rut, and I had to grab Dad's arm.

"Do I have a talent?"

"Yes. You have a talent for driving me and your mother insane."

The next day was Mom's birthday. In the afternoon, Grandma gave me a dollar bill. Mom protested and said it wasn't necessary. I held the bill in my hand, turning it over to look at each side. Mom didn't allow me to have money.

"Jay, go to the variety store and give your mother a rest. Better yet, go find Percival. You two can go together. Here's a dollar for him."

Percival and I walked on Lake Street toward the center of town. We stopped in front of the hospital and sat on a bench. I gave Percival his dollar. He pulled another one from his pocket and held them up to show me.

I held my dollar up, so it fluttered in the breeze. "I only have one. I'm getting candy cigarettes and Miracle Bubbles. What are you going to get?"

"A Hot Wheels car."

A bell clanged when we entered the variety store. Next to the entrance was a rocket ship gumball machine. To the left was a soda fountain with six empty stools in front of a counter that concealed humming ice cream freezers. To the right was a candy display. In the back of the store, the pharmacist, Mr. Peck, better known as "Pecker" among the boys he'd coached in hockey, scraped pills into a bottle.

I pointed at the candy rack. "Let's take some."

"Are you kidding? We'll get caught."

I grabbed three candy bars, stuffed them into my left front pocket and pointed at the blocks of gum on the bottom shelf. Percival grabbed a handful and pushed them into his right front pocket. I took three rolls of Life Savers and shoved them into my left rear pocket. Percival did the same. We continued toward the pharmacy counter, around the end cap and into the toy aisle. I picked up a bottle of Miracle Bubbles. Percival lifted a green Land Rover from a rod holding Matchbox cars. Back in the candy aisle, we each took a pack of candy cigarettes.

"You boys finished?" A reflection of Pecker, hunched over the rear counter, loomed in the mirror above the door.

"Yes," I said.

Pecker loped down the steps from the platform to the cash register. We paid for the bubbles, the car and the cigarettes. The floorboards squeaked as we walked out. I was certain the noise signaled our theft. Once outside, we ran down Lake Street toward Grandpa's house. I suggested we go to City Park to blow bubbles.

I stepped up onto the top of a picnic table. A fresh breeze off the lake cooled my face. I pulled out the wand and blew into it. A line of bubbles emerged from the ring. The wind caught them, carrying them into the elm branches.

"Hey, they put an extra wand in," I said.

Percival got up on the table and took the second wand. I spun around so that a ring of bubbles formed, and Percival followed my lead. The bubbles surrounded us in dual spirals that mixed, separated and collided. We got dizzy, bumping into each other; the spirals became tornadoes. Our backs slammed together, and we tumbled off the table into the grass. We remained there, watching the bubbles slowly rise and burst, until the last one disappeared.

The next morning Dad and I waited at the fishery with Moose and Jim. They smiled when Uncle Lance, Percival and Grandpa stepped onto the dock.

Lance shook the big man's hand first.

"Moose, good to see you."

"When was the last time you were out?"

"1958."

"Fifteen years? It's hard to believe."

"Jim, good to see you." Lance shook Jim's hand. "Moose. Jim. This is my son Percival."

Percival's hand looked like a toy in Moose's grip. "I've been working with your grandpa since your dad was your age." He laughed and tapped Percival's back. "Out here to learn the family business?"

Percival looked at Lance, not sure what to say. Lance said he wanted him to see what he did growing up. Jim handed him a pair of green waders like mine.

"It's the best way to be—out on the water. You can leave your troubles ashore."

"He's got plenty of troubles." Lance turned to Percival. "Put those waders on."

"Your Dad had plenty of troubles to leave on shore too, so don't worry," Moose said. "You'll feel better at the end of the day."

"What happened when you got back to Grandpa's house?" I asked Percival. He told me as we made our way out to the nets.

G randma asked Percival what he got with the dollar she had given him. He showed her the Land Rover.

Aunt Gwen leaned forward on the couch. "What did Jay get?"

"Bubbles."

"Did you get anything else?"

"No."

"What's in your pockets?"

"Nothing."

"Show me."

Percival pulled out the Bazookas and Life Savers and set them on the coffee table.

"Did you pay for those?"

He looked up at her, watching the skin around her mouth tighten and her eyes narrow.

"Jay made me do it! He said to take them."

"Pardon us." Gwen grabbed him by the ear, led him down the stairs to the side entry, and pushed him into the garage. "You have embarrassed us to no end. You're going to return those things and apologize."

Lance came through the broken door. "What's he done now?"

"Stolen candy."

"I swear, you are a little shit." Lance grabbed him by the shoulder with one hand and the back of his pants with the other. "Get the pink stick."

"Jay made me do it. It's his fault. I wouldn't have done it otherwise."

"You're going to learn responsibility, even if I have to beat it into you through your ass."

Gwen returned with the stick, which was the handle of a toy mop Aoife had been given for her birthday. She handed it to Lance. Percival said he could hear the swoosh of it whipping through the air before it hit him. When Lance raised the stick for the next one, Percival said he hated them both. The stick came down harder. He tried to kick Lance's shins before the next one, but he missed and lost his balance.

Percival punched my arm. "I'm going to get you for this. It's your fault." He sat on his hands with his arms stiff. I couldn't get him to talk anymore.

Dad piloted the boat while Lance, Grandpa and Moose smoked in the bow. Jim pulled us out of the pilothouse. He took us to the stern and showed us how to measure nautical speed using a reel, a watch and a knotted line.

"These guys might be real sailors someday," Jim said to Lance and Grandpa as they came to the stern.

The boat slowed. Grandpa told me and Percival to sit in the back of the pilothouse and keep out of the way while they lifted the net.

We sat on a bench under the rifle, facing the stern, where we could see out the doors on either side. Dad and Lance had their backs to us. On the up swells, they pulled the net over the gunwale. On the down swells, they pushed the net toward the deck. Percival craned his neck out the door to see them working. A couple times, the gunwale tipped below the trough, allowing water to pour over the side. Percival yelled at Lance, asking if we were going to tip over. He said not to worry, we weren't going to capsize. Grandpa built the best wooden boats on the lake.

Dad poked his head in.

"Jay, teach Percival how to tie a bowline. You may need to secure mooring lines while we move boxes."

I took a short piece of rope from a hook near the life jackets. I held it on my lap and formed a twisted loop with the ends extending over my thighs.

"First you form the tree and the hole. Then, the rabbit goes around the tree and down the hole."

On the way to the next net, after many attempts, Percival managed to tie one right. Grandpa asked if we wanted to do the mooring lines when we got there. I said yes. Lance took Percival to the stern, while Jim took me to the bow. Lance told Percival if he got this right, he'd be on his way to becoming a true lake man. I saw no chance of that happening.

Lance positioned him in the starboard corner of the stern and told him to hold the line with both hands. When the stake approached, he stood behind him, holding his elbows.

"Reach out like you're going to hug the piling. Wrap the line around it, form the loop and finish the knot. Make sure your arms don't get caught between the boat and the piling."

Every time I handled a mooring line, I had a vision of my arm getting crushed and turned into a ribbon like a cartoon character. Jim stood behind me.

"Here it comes. Try to time when you put your arms out to the top of the swell." His grip on my arms was tight. The boat slid down and started back up toward the crest.

"Now."

I reached out, and Jim pushed my arms forward, flinging my right hand so the doubled-over end of the line wrapped around the piling. My left hand caught the line by instinct. Jim tapped my shoulder. "That was perfect, you let the rope come to your hand."

I twisted the rope to form a loop and sent the rabbit around the cleated line. Jim pointed to the hole. "Now put it through and draw the line tight."

I tried to pull, but the tension was too high. The boat slid down the next wave. I jerked the line again. The knot snapped into place when the boat rose.

Grandpa patted me on the back.

"Son, he's already better than you were."

I looked to the stern. Lance smiled. "This one's a sea dog. I didn't have to help him at all." Percival squinted at me through wet hair splayed over his eyes.

"Time for you boys to sit down," Dad said. "We'll see who can finish the fastest on the last net."

"Two dollars says Jay is quicker," Jim said.

"I'll take that," Moose said. "I'm going with Percival. He's rough, but he's got heart."

"Arthur, you're the judge. We can't expect the fathers to be fair," Jim winked at me. Grandpa nodded and smiled.

We practiced using the coat hooks inside the pilothouse. I was quicker than Percival, but my knots were loose. On the last net, we switched positions, with Percival and Moose in the bow and Jim and me in the stern, while Grandpa stood in the center of the starboard side. The swells tapered. Dad brought the boat up to the stakes in a perfect glide.

"Go!" Grandpa yelled.

The gunwale bounced into a piling, followed by a loud splash.

Jim hollered at me, "Percival dropped his line."

I fumbled mine looking to see what happened.

"Hurry, hurry, Jay lost his grip," Moose yelled.

I still managed to catch the loop around the piling and finish a loose knot.

Percival flung his line around again; this time he caught the end and drew the line tight. Jim and I watched Percival finish.

"Jay wins," Grandpa said. "Well done, Percival. Jay's had a lot more practice than you."

"Percival, you tied a better knot," Moose said. "You need to go faster."

We went out on the lake the next two days. I loved it. Riding in the boat, watching the seagulls, tying the knots. On the first day out, off Buffalo Point, Dad told me what I thought was the full story of how he lost his leg. On the second day out, off Elm Point, he told me how a guy jumped overboard to swim to Canada, and that I might see him if I looked hard enough.

On the last net, Percival tied his line faster than me. Moose said it was about time, and he expected Percival to bring him two dollars next time he was in town. Dad came out of the pilothouse to start lifting. "Shake hands, boys."

I looked at Percival. The spot where the baseball hit my lip still hurt like hell. Percival extended his arm, and I shook his hand. I asked him if he could come back in the fall. He looked at Lance. "Sure, maybe for Labor Day or Thanksgiving, if you boys apologize to Mr. Peck at the drug store."

And I'd thought we'd left our troubles ashore.

Twelve: September 1974

Dad carried the gun in its case. I carried a canvas bag filled with old bottles. In the field among clusters of discarded mink-farm equipment surrounded by tall grass and wild raspberry bushes, sat two old Buicks filled with cardboard boxes, a collapsed boat hull and a weathered dining room table with six chairs. Every summer, hornets infested the hull. Now, a few late-September survivors buzzed around the pilothouse. The smell of the freshly cut grass mixed with the sour plume from the mink sheds and rotting raspberries. Dad put the gun on the table. He told me to set up the bottles.

I stomped through twenty-five yards of stiff weeds and brown grass to get to the target rack. Dad said Wayne built the rack with three levels to hold each shape of his favorite beer bottles. On the right side he'd mounted an iron hook to hang whatever odd item he thought would be fun to use for target practice. On the day I learned to shoot, a bedpan dangled on the hook.

As I finished inserting bottles into the rack's holes, I saw Wayne's truck jounce its way out to the table. Grandpa, Wayne, and Lance were inside, and Percival and Will were in the truck box, sitting on the wheel wells, hurling dirt clods at each other and laughing while the wind pushed their hair back. I hung my head on the way back to the table, wishing the others hadn't shown up.

Dad looked at me and shrugged. "I wanted it to be just you and me, but Grandpa wanted all of you to learn together." He massaged my shoulders. "We'll come again by ourselves to practice."

I kicked a bunch of the cut grass that lay around the table. It exploded in a puff and flew off in the breeze.

They came in a wave from the pickup. Lance plunked two brown paper bags on the table. "Here's your dinner. We had ours before we left."

Dad took one of the bags, crumpling the top with his hand. Percival and I sat down at the end of the table. Grandpa put his gun case down next to Dad's and set a case of 20-gauge target shells next to it.

Lance pointed toward me. "He doesn't look too happy."

"We had a busy morning."

Dad settled on a chair. "Lance, when's the last time you fired a weapon?"

"Twenty years ago, in the Army. I qualified as an Expert."

Grandpa unzipped the case with the 20 gauge. He took the gun out and handed it to Lance. "Remember this?"

"Sure, I brought down my first birds with it." He looked at the stock, cradling it. "It's got a firm kick if I remember right."

"It does, but I think the boys can handle it."

Lance walked over to the firing line, an oval patch of dirt a few steps from the table. In a fluid motion, he swung the weapon up to his right shoulder and aimed at an imaginary bird flying right to left. He said the gun felt heavier than he remembered and lowered it, pointing the barrel to the ground.

Dad made a quacking sound. "Not bad, but you missed."

"His arms don't get much work pushing paper," Wayne added.

Grandpa pushed his hat back on his head. "I bet he can outshoot both of you."

"Pete, that sounds like a challenge," Wayne said. "Once the boys are done, I think we ought to have a little contest. Don't you?"

"Yup. Lance, you in?"

"I don't know…"

Percival slapped the tabletop. "Dad, you're better than them."

I pushed Percival off his chair. "No way, my dad is better."

"I'm going to beat you all." Grandpa raised his hands to the back of his head.

Wayne crossed his arms. "I guess we're going to see if the great Sir Lancelot really can be defeated."

We lined up in the bare patch, three feet apart. Wayne stood in front of us with Dad's 12 gauge. He showed us how to tell if the safety was on and how to hold the gun. He demonstrated how to keep the first finger behind the trigger until it was time to fire.

Grandpa handed the 20 gauge to me. My arms sank under the unexpected weight.

"I didn't think it would be this heavy. They look light on TV."

Dad shifted in his chair. "What you see on TV is bullshit."

We took turns following through the process with the 20 gauge. On the last time through, it slipped through Percival's hands when I handed it to him. It fell butt first into the grass, giving me a direct view down the barrel.

Wayne shook his head. "If that happened with the gun loaded and the safety off, one of you would be dead."

I picked up the gun and checked the safety. "I guess I'm still alive."

Honking from a vee of Canada geese drifted across the field. Grandpa walked up and stood behind us. A splash came from the river when the geese landed. "Are we gonna shoot now?" Percival said.

Lance grabbed him by the shoulder. "You'll shoot when we say so."

"Dad, do you have a plug in the magazine?" Wayne said.

"Yes," Grandpa replied.

"Good. I've got one too. Lance, gimme three shells."

Wayne loaded two shells in the magazine and one in the chamber. He clicked off the safety and swung the weapon up to his shoulder. He fired three quick shots, breaking a bottle each time. A smoldering shell flew out of the ejection port after each shot.

Will jumped back. "That was so cool."

"Yeah, those bottles just blew up!" The explosions amazed me.

Percival tilted his head toward Lance. "Is that what happens when you shoot a bird?"

"No, the shot tears the bird's flesh, and it falls into the water in one piece."

Wayne made a splashing sound and lowered his weapon.

"These are semi-automatic shotguns. That means you have to pull the trigger for each shot, and you don't have to reload. After each shot, a new shell is loaded into the chamber. The weapon is ready to fire and dangerous until the magazine is empty. Understand?" We nodded. "Now, before you can shoot, you need to learn to do the swing."

Lance grinned. "I didn't know you were going to teach them to dance."

Dad laughed and kicked one of the chairs over.

"What's so damn funny, Cap'n Ahab? Your dancing days are long over." The smile left Dad's face as Wayne spoke. "How about this? We're going to learn to bring the gun into firing position. Is that okay, Sir Lancelot?"

Lance flung his hands up and rolled his eyes. "I used to think you had a sense of humor."

"I did until I started sending part of my hard-earned money to your sorry ass for nothing." Wayne stepped toward Lance.

"And every year the amount you send gets smaller." Lance stepped toward Wayne.

"Hey, if you're so unsatisfied, take your kid and get the hell out of here."

Grandpa stepped between them. "No one's going anywhere. Now let's get back to shooting. I'd like to have a nice afternoon with my sons and grandkids."

I turned to face Lance at the table and the barrel of the gun pointed at him. "We didn't want you here. We wanted to come out here ourselves."

Lance raised his eyebrows.

Wayne grabbed the barrel, pushing it toward the ground. "Jay, pay attention to where you're pointing the weapon at all times. And that goes for all of you. I don't want to have to clean up some mess because one of you was careless. Got that?"

We murmured yes and shuffled our feet in the dirt. Wayne took in a deep breath, blew it out hard, and picked up where he'd left off: bringing the gun into firing position, aiming and loading.

"When you're hunting, you're allowed three shells. You can have two in the magazine and one in the chamber." Wayne pointed to the wood grip below the barrel to show us the magazine. He pointed to the chamber through the port in the right side of the receiver. "The gun can hold five shells, but when you're hunting, you have to put a plug in the magazine that takes up the space of two shells to hunt legally. I don't ever want to get a visit from the game warden telling me he caught one of you boys with five shells, because they check. Got it?"

Wayne asked each of us directly if we understood. We said yes.

Turning the weapon sideways, Wayne inserted two shells into the magazine by pushing them into the port on the bottom of the gun. He attempted to push in a third shell, and it wouldn't go past the carrier.

"This is what the game warden will do. He'll try to put a third shell into the magazine. If it goes in, you're busted. If not, you're legal. Understand?"

We nodded.

"We're almost ready to shoot. Will, you're going first. Now remember, until you're ready to fire, make sure the safety is on."

Will pulled back the bolt, inserted a shell in the chamber, and let the bolt slide forward. Wayne pointed at the trigger.

"Is the safety on?"

"Yes."

"I'm going to count down from three. When I get to one, I want you to swing the weapon into firing position and shoot the three bottles in the lower left of the rack. Okay? And be ready for the recoil, because it will hurt a little."

"Okay."

"Now slide the safety to the off position."

Wayne started the countdown at the click of the safety.

"Three. Two. One."

Will hit the first bottle and missed high with the other two shots. Splinters flew off the front of the rack.

"That was awesome, but the kick hurts."

"You'll get used to it. Percival, you're next."

He planted his feet and loaded.

"Ready?"

He nodded.

Wayne gave him the countdown. Moments after he said "one," three bottles shattered: the two bottles Will missed, plus the adjacent one. Percival looked at Lance with a surprised look on his face.

"Good job."

"I'm going to have a bruise on my shoulder." Percival handed the gun to me. "Aim just below the target."

"Don't bug me. Just watch how it's done."

I set up in the bare patch and loaded. Wayne gave me the countdown. The fifth bottle on the second tier exploded. I shifted and fired. The top of the sixth bottle came off with a ragged edge and the bottom remained intact. I fired again and the rest fell in pieces.

Dad lit a cigarette. "You don't get a second chance at a duck. They fly out of range."

We took turns shooting for the next hour. Percival missed once in thirty shots. Will struggled with going high because he didn't anticipate the kick. The smell of burned gunpowder drifted over the grass. I fired at the bedpan to hear the noise.

When Wayne told us it was the adults' turn to shoot, we grumbled, slouched over to the table, and flopped onto the chairs. Wayne asked which gun they should use for the contest.

Grandpa adjusted his hat. "Let's use the 20 gauge. We all learned to shoot with it."

Wayne turned to Dad. "You okay with that?"

"Sure. Jay, go set up some targets."

I went to the rack to set up the bottles. Dad brought two boxes of shells to the patch. I overheard Dad while I loaded the rack.

"What are we going to do about Brigitte Bardot and that animal rights crowd?"

"I know what I'd like to do about Brigitte Bardot." Wayne held up his shotgun and grabbed his crotch. "This one's for killin' and this one's for fun."

"I can't believe I'm related to you." Lance massaged his temples.

"Don't tell me you wouldn't want to get your hands on that."

"Those days are gone, brother." Lance finally cracked a slight smile. "Pete's the ladies' man. Problem is, he never knew it before he got married, and now it's too late."

"I'm sure I could give her a better run than those French husbands she's had." Dad hadn't completely lost it. "But seriously, what are we going to do? We can't let this go on."

"I think she should stick to *Playboy* and the movies," Wayne said. "Anybody want a beer?"

Dad raised his hand. "Sure, I'll have one."

"Will, how about if you go to the workshop and get four bottles out of the fridge." Will put his head down on the table. Wayne dispensed with the nice approach. "Go. Now."

Will got up and started toward the building. The shadows from the poplar and willow trees near the river were creeping onto the field, and shading the target rack. Grandpa picked up the shell casings from behind the patch and put them in the empty bottle bag.

"Pelt sales are down 20 percent the last three years. Prices are down too. We've got to figure out a way to stop it."

Wayne held the gun out to Grandpa. "You want to shoot first?"

"Sure. Lance, three turns sound good?"

"You might need more to catch me."

"Three turns will be enough for me to beat you. Unless Cap'n Ahab gets lucky."

"Don't push it, Wayne. You haven't had any beer yet."

Grandpa walked to the patch. He swung the weapon up and the lower right bottle shattered. The bottle to the left collapsed with the next shot. On the third, the center right bottle collapsed in the middle, the bottom shattering when it hit the ground.

"Old Man, three. Sons, zero."

He handed the gun to Lance.

"The ranchers association is going to try a new ad campaign to counter the animal activists, but that won't be enough. I've got to figure out a way to transfer the fishing licenses. Right now, the state won't allow transfer or inheritance by family members. The license expires with the holder. If we can't maintain a low-cost feed supply, all the pelt sales in the world won't matter, because we'll be taping a dollar bill to every pelt we ship."

Lance loaded and fired three shots. The bottles on the lower right side of the rack collapsed in quick succession. "Maybe I still have it. Dad, you going to St. Paul in January for the next session?"

"No, I'm gonna wait. See how the '76 election turns out. Maybe we can make some contributions and get someone more amenable to our cause."

Will returned with the beers. Grandpa took out his pocketknife and uncapped the bottles. Will sat down, away from Percival and me. Wayne sat next to Will.

"Ready, Pete?"

I looked at the others. "You can beat them Dad. They're no good."

Dad set his beer down in the grass and limped from the table to the patch. He looked down the barrel at the ground. "You need to fix the license transfer problem. If you don't, we'll all be working at Worland's." He swung the gun up, fired, hit the upper right bottle, and missed the other two low. "Fuck, now I'm distracted."

Wayne walked to the patch. "I'll work in the Number Two, paint houses or drive a school bus, but I'll never work for those people." He set his feet and loaded the gun. He hit the first two and pulled the last shot high. "Damnit, all this shit is throwing me off."

Grandpa folded his hands in front of him on the table. "Mary is one of those people."

"That makes it worse."

Each of us cheered our fathers on. Grandpa missed high on his third shot, and Lance made it through the second round without a miss. All of them had a clean third round, which made Lance the winner. He remained the only one to beat Grandpa in a shooting contest.

The sun fell below the trees. I said I wanted to see a full bottle shot, so they lined up their half-finished beers on top of the rack. I gave each of them a single shell.

"It's bad luck if you miss."

Grandpa shattered the first bottle and we cheered. Lance's shot was high but took off the top of the second, leaving a ragged cup. Wayne hit his square in the middle, creating an explosion of foam. We hollered again. Dad took his position in the patch, swung the gun up and fired.

The shot sailed left.

Thirteen: July 1976

The summer after we learned to shoot, Lance's family came to Worland for Independence Day weekend. On the morning of the third, Dad burst into my room to wake me up. He stood there until I finished the last button on my shirt. I pushed past him and headed for the kitchen. My hunger roared once I'd fully woken up. I gobbled down two eggs and toast Mom made for me, while Dad packed our lunches and filled a small cooler from the freezer.

At the fishery, Grandpa, Lance and Percival stood on the dock. Below the crane, four fish boxes sat under a canvas tarp. Dad extended his hand to Lance.

"It's about time you got back to doing real work."

"It's good to remind myself why I work with my brain rather than my back."

Percival walked over to me. He waved awkwardly.

"Good morning, Pete," Grandpa said.

"You okay?"

"I've been better."

"Where are we going today?" Lance said.

"Elm Point," Dad replied.

"What's under the tarp?"

"You'll find out soon enough."

"Where are Moose and Jim?"

"Moose had to stop. His back gave out."

"What about Jim?"

"He works when he wants to. He's got his Navy pension."

"So, it's you and Dad…and Jay? What about Wayne?"

"Wayne has his hands full with the ranch and his kids. We've got another guy who helps out."

"Do I know him?"

"No, he's not from around here."

Percival and Lance found oilers and boots in the fishery while Dad and Grandpa lowered the tarp-covered fish boxes on board. I boarded last, after handing down our lunch boxes. Dad started the engine, and we moved out into the river.

The water was calm. Percival and I sat on fish boxes in the bow; Grandpa stood next to us. Once we were on the open lake, the wind created a three-foot chop. The channel markers' flashing red beacons receded until they vanished from the horizon.

Forty minutes later, the nets and pilings off Elm Point came into view. An aluminum runabout tied to one of the pilings rolled on the waves. A man wearing a camouflage jacket sat on the center bench of the small boat.

"Who is that?" Lance said.

Grandpa took the helm. Lance followed Dad to the bow. He tossed a hitched loop over the same piling. The man stepped from his boat into ours.

"Lance, this is Roger Fixx."

He shook Roger's hand. "You're the—"

"Yes," Roger said.

"You live out here?"

"I've got an old camper, a good rifle and all the fish I can eat." He smiled and slapped Dad on the back. "What more could I want?"

"Do you think Carter will really pardon you guys if he wins? He's ex-Navy, you know."

"I hope he does. I've been laying low for ten years."

Roger and Dad transferred food, beer, a bundle of newspapers and some paperback books from the covered fish boxes into the small boat. After emptying the last box, Dad set the cooler on top of the stack. Roger secured the tarp over the goods. "What's in the cooler?"

"Ice." Dad hooked his thumbs on the straps of his oilers. "And a couple steaks. Wish I could sit out here and eat one with you tonight."

I untied the bow line. We drifted away from the piling. Grandpa piloted the boat to the other side of the pound. On the way, Dad asked Percival if he remembered how to tie mooring lines. It had been a year since the knot contest. He tartly said that he did.

Lance went to the stern with Percival and stood behind him. Roger followed. The poplar leaves on Elm Point shimmered in the breeze. The shore looked the same as the year before, when I learned to tie a mooring line. It probably looked the same as twenty years before that when Dad started out, and forty years before that when Grandpa Ciaran and the Indians fished there.

Percival got the line around the piling and pulled the end through the twisted loop to form a tight knot. We lined up on the starboard side. Grandpa sat on a fish box, smoking his pipe. Roger and Dad loosened the tunnel lines. We all reached over the side to grab the net. Dad reached into his breast pocket and ate two aspirins. Silver and green fish slid out of the bunched net onto the deck.

Roger, with his long beard and greasy ponytail, looked like the French voyageurs I saw in my history book.

"What are you going to do if Carter pardons you guys?" Lance asked.

"Maybe go to law school. My family won't talk to me. I've thought about staying here, maybe move into town, but I'm not sure how long this will last."

Dad shuffle through the accumulating fish on the deck to get to the dipper controls. "Jay. Percival. Get out of the way, we're going to start bailing."

Roger removed the dipper from its rack and guided it into the water. We sat in the pilothouse while Lance went to the bow next to Grandpa, who was still sitting on a fish box smoking his pipe.

"Dad, what are you going to do?" Lance said.

"I'm going to St. Paul in January. I need to transfer the license to Pete. If I can't get the state to reverse the transfer ban, we're done." He kicked a flopping tullibee. "We'll be no better off than that fish."

"Pete could work with Wayne at the ranch. They've got all their boys to help. They could do it."

Grandpa took the pipe out of his mouth and stood up. He thrust his face close to Lance's.

"Don't bullshit me. Pete would never work with Wayne at the ranch. The fact is, we've got half the mink we had ten years ago. Those goddamn celebrities and animal rights people have made sure of that. They don't know shit about raising animals, or my right to make a decent living, let alone how to make a decent movie. You know, Ginny and I went to see *Taxi Driver* last weekend and we walked out. Is that what passes for entertainment now? Watching our society disintegrate?"

"Dad, things aren't going well for anyone these days. You got through the Depression, the war and all the rest. You'll get through this."

"I don't know. It's different. I used to feel like people and the government wanted us to succeed. Now it seems like they want us out of the way."

Lance took over guiding the dipper from Roger. Roger sat in the pilothouse under the rifle, taking a few minutes out of the sun.

"Dad, why did you leave?" Percival said. "This is fun. I want to do this when I grow up."

Dad looked at Lance from behind the dipper controls. Roger craned his neck around the front of the pilothouse. Grandpa rolled the stem of his pipe in his fingers.

"You're going to college," Lance barked. "You need to get an education. Work with your mind."

Percival tilted his head, looking at Lance from under the bill of his hat. His arms hung at his sides. "What if I want to do this?"

Grandpa got up and stood behind Roger.

I adjusted my oilers. "We could do it together."

Grandpa looked out at Elm Point as if he wished to escape there as Roger had. Dad pushed on the top fish box to align it with the ones below, while keeping his left hand on the dipper controls. Roger put two boxes on top of the stack.

"You have to go after what you want in life," Roger said. "It won't wait, and it might disappear while you're going after it."

It was one thing to come to Worland a couple times a year and go out on the lake. It was quite another to have to go out nearly every day from April until November. Lance told Percival he wanted him to know who he came from and what they did. I could tell Lance wanted Percival's life separate from Worland, as he had separated himself. I also knew Dad didn't care what Lance wanted.

"Boys, you can work out here as much and as long as you like. Now let's get that dipper back in the water."

After we finished lifting the second net, we dropped Roger off at his boat. Dad handed him three walleyes in a plastic bag.

"You going to the fireworks tomorrow?"

"Nah, I don't feel like celebrating." He put the bag under the tarp. "Thanks, Pete."

"Jay, untie Roger's line."

The boat drifted away from the piling. Roger came about, powered up and headed toward shore. We rolled gently in his wake. Gulls rose off the pilings, taking flight in a swirl. The small craft became a speck on the water, and the vee behind it spread out on either side of us until the vast lake absorbed it.

Fourteen: October 1976

All the public schools in Minnesota close on a Thursday and Friday in mid-October for a teacher's convention. I invited Percival to come to Worland from the Cities for the long weekend. To this day, I remember the weight of the phone receiver in my right hand as I suggested we could help Dad bring in the nets and go duck hunting. We met Lance and Percival in Bemidji at the Paul Bunyan statue. Dad and Lance waved to each other while Percival ran from his car to ours.

We arrived in Worland late Thursday afternoon and went to see Grandma and Grandpa. Grandma stood up from the couch when we came in. A paisley bandanna shrouded her head. Three strained bursts of sound came from her mouth when she tried to speak. She shook her head, then put her arms around me. I thought she might break when I hugged her.

After dinner, I asked Mom if we could go to the movies. She gave us five dollars and told us to come straight home. We got to the theater early. At the candy counter, I got Dots. Percival got Junior Mints. We sat in the middle of a row near the back. Small groups of kids sat scattered around the theater. As Percival put a mint into his mouth, I grabbed his wrist.

"What are you doing?"

"I'm having a mint."

"You need to save those."

"For what?"

I reached into my box of candy and held up a piece for him to see, then lobbed it toward three girls seated ten rows in front of us. It passed through the house lights like a meteor, landing between a ponytailed blond and a perfectly combed brunette. They looked to see where the projectile might have come from, while their friend with a messy bob leaned in to hear what they were saying.

"Your turn," I whispered. "You're the great ball player. This should be easy."

A questioning look passed over his face, like why throw perfectly good mints instead of eating them, and what form of trouble will this bring. He had no sense of fun. The stage lights turned the girls' heads into silhouettes, making them easy targets. Since bob had not turned around after the first toss, he aimed for her. She leaned across the brunette to say something to ponytail and then leaned back. Percival let it fly. The mint hit bob in the back-left side of her head, ricocheted into the lap of the brunette, and tumbled to the floor. Bob turned around, got her bearings and spotted him. I thought she was going to wave. Instead, a handful of Jawbreakers rained down on us. I fired off a Dot that overshot the girls and hit a letterman sitting with his date three rows beyond. He stood up and returned fire with M&Ms, a couple of which hit the girls in between, and sat back down.

The screen filled with light and the cackle of Woody Woodpecker burst out from the speakers. Sprays of flying candy filled the projection beam from all directions. It pinged the seats in front of us. Playful screams from the girls curled up the walls and flowed down the aisles. Candy hit the screen, causing waves to ripple through the bodies of Woody and his pals as they chased each other around a tree. Percival ducked behind the seat back. I flung candy over the top. A hand tugged on Percival's arm. It was bob. She ran her hand through his hair, kissed him on the cheek, and darted out of the row in a crouch. Ponytail did the same to me. The cartoon stopped. The theater went black. The house lights clicked on, catching bob mid-stride in the aisle. She froze. A man strode in from the exit behind her. A Jawbreaker clinked against the seat in front of me and rolled to a stop.

"If this happens again, I'm going to stop the show. No refunds."
There was murmuring and shuffling in the seats. "I'm not kidding."

He turned and walked out. Unfreezing herself, bob dashed back to her seat, where she turned and waved. Percival fluttered his fingers at her. I couldn't tell if she really liked him, or if it was a girl's cruelty to an inept boy. The theater went dark, and the cartoon resumed, the sound whooshing up to speed. I leaned into Percival with a Dot in my hand.

"That's Bernice Fitzgerald. She's in my English class. Do you like her?"

He took the Dot from my hand, a confused look on his face.

"Girls at my school don't do that—or throw candy." I stared at him, waiting for a comment on Bernice.

"She's cute."

"Maybe we'll see them on Sunday. They go to our church."

After the show, we walked to Grandpa's under a cold, moonless sky. The elm trees cast long shadows in the streetlights. I pulled the hood of my sweatshirt over my head.

"We're going duck hunting tomorrow morning. Come over at five-thirty."

"Is Uncle Pete coming with us?"

"No, Dad has to lift nets with Roger tomorrow."

"Isn't it against the law for us to hunt without an adult?"

"Will is coming with. He's seventeen and has a license. We'll be okay."

"Are you sure?"

"It's our only chance to go. Dad and Wayne are hunting on Saturday."

I also told him the game warden patrolled the Northwest Angle on Fridays, so we wouldn't get caught.

Dad kept the duck boat on a wood slip next to the fishery. Will climbed in first, put the gun next to the oars, and sat on the bow seat. He told Percival to get in next and sit on the middle bench. I climbed in last. Will and I used the oars to shove off. We drifted out from the landing toward the channel markers on the opposite side of the river. The red beacons flashed every few seconds. I pulled the ripcord and the engine gurgled to life.

We headed northeast out of the river's mouth, past the Number Two and around the end of the jetty, on to the lake. A slice of orange sun lined the horizon below heavy clouds. On the short trip along the marshy shore to the duck blind, Will yelled over the rumble of the motor that the birds would fly south on their way to the reeds near the channel markers. They might land for a rest north of the blind. Since we weren't going to set decoys, he figured we might get two or three opportunities to catch birds moving from north to south across the river.

I slowed the boat, following Will's direction into the marsh. The red and yellow leaves on shore turned luminous as the clouds broke and the sun hit them. Tall, thick reeds hid us from the water and the sky. Will tied the mooring line to a piling driven into the mud. The bow pointed north, and we faced east toward the lake. I took the gun out of its case and handed it to Percival.

"Ready to shoot, city slicker?"

It was the Remington Model 11 we had learned to shoot with two years before. Grandpa had given it to me for my birthday. Will handed Percival three shells. He put two in the magazine and one in the chamber, each with a firm click.

"Watch how it's done."

We sat quietly for about half an hour, while the sun rose into a gathering overcast. A breath of wind sent a ripple across the open water. To the north, we heard a burst of splashing. Murmured quacks drifted over us. Will put his hand on Percival's shoulder.

"Northeast, a hundred feet."

He turned to locate the sound. There were five mallards paddling around, dipping their bills. I surveyed the reeds to anticipate their flight path. It started as a slow rustling and built into a full rush of splashing wings. They came up in a line, low over the vegetation, forty feet away, heading toward the river. A light rain began to fall. Percival swung the gun into firing position and pulled the trigger. The blast broke the tranquility of feathers moving in still air. He missed the lead male. Following his sight line, he got the third one with the second shot. The fifth one, his head a luminous green in the morning sun, came within range low over the reeds. I heard a squeak and a rattle, then the explosion of the shot. A force as if some giant paddle had slammed into my right arm sent me spinning. I tried to stop, certain that I'd become detached from all that held me to the world. I couldn't breathe. Then, amid the spinning, a moment where the ascending ducks froze over the channel markers in perfect focus. The spinning resumed. I fell, and the impact shocked me into breathing. I heard Will and Percival shout at each other. I came to sprawled over the rear bench on my back; certain I'd slammed my arm into the motor while following the flight of the last bird. My right arm felt wet and sore. I sat up. A bolt of pain shot through my shoulder. I reached over with my left hand to touch my arm.

"Don't touch it!" The boat rocked violently as Will scrambled around Percival to get to me. "Don't look." He grabbed me around the chest. I thought my shoulder had separated from my body. It hung loose. I couldn't control it. He dragged me to the middle bench next to Percival. The gun slipped out of his hand and rattled into the bilge.

"Percival! Cut the mooring line!"

Will let go. I looked down. The sleeve of my jacket was shredded and soaked from the elbow down. I couldn't tell from the mess what remained. Will grabbed me again, spinning me around to face the bow. He tied the mooring line around the top of my arm, sending lightning through my shoulder.

Percival stared at me, as if someone had hit him on the head with a hammer. The rain grew heavy. Will piloted the boat around the jetty, past the Number Two and up the river, toward the hospital dock. Each wave we crashed through sent a shock of pain through my shoulder into my chest. I grew faint. The oily fumes from the engine accelerated my nausea, until I vomited on my boots. Rusty bilge water washed over my feet.

This can't be happening.

This can't be happening.

When the boat hit the dock pilings, I saw my index finger drift out from under the bench, floating in the bilge. My lungs started to heave beyond my control. I vomited again. Will scrambled onto the dock. He told Percival to keep me conscious while he ran across the street to the hospital. Urine leaked into my pants. Dad didn't tell me about that happening when they'd brought him in.

Then nothing.

Fifteen: October 1976

I saw my mother's bloodshot eyes first. Swollen lids with cracked mascara drooped over them. I lingered in a twilight state until they came into focus. Near the window, Dad sat with a blank expression on his face. My heart tightened into a fist.

Pain in my right arm jolted me awake. I reached across my chest to touch it, but Mom grabbed my left hand and held it with both of hers.

"It's not there, sweetheart."

"I can feel it."

I tilted my head. White gauze wrapping covered my arm, but the end barely reached my chest. It looked more like a wing than an arm. An electric sensation moved through my muscles. My chest heaved. I tried to sit up and thrashed in the tangled bedding.

"That bastard Percival! I'm going to kill him. I swear! Mom–"

She grabbed my shoulders. Tears flooded my eyes and dribbled down my face. I sank into the mattress and forced the air out of my lungs. She wiped my eyes.

"Settle down sweetheart. Please relax." Her lips drew tight. Black streaks formed under her eyes.

"Where is he? Is he still around?"

"He's still here," Dad said. "Lance drove all night to come and get him. I don't know when they plan to head back to the Cities."

"Are they going to come here?"

"We told them not to until we see how you're doing."

"How does it look like he's doing?" Mom said. "How could you let this happen?"

"What? This is my fault? Percival shot him."

"You let them go out there by themselves."

"Hey, you didn't speak up when I said it was okay."

"You should have gone with Jay and Percival. Will can barely manage himself. Instead, you let them go unsupervised so you could hunt with Wayne."

Dad stared at her while his face reddened. "I just wanted them to have fun together. Have some time away from school and adults. That's all."

"Well, that turned out great, didn't it?" Mom headed to the door. "Let's go. He needs to rest, and I have to make my rounds. Sweetheart, we'll be back this afternoon."

The fist in my chest unwound. I drifted back to sleep in the billowy sheets.

Will came in after lunch, shoulders slouched and reeking of mink. He flopped into the chair next to the window. A long blade of grass stuck out of his thick blond hair. He'd inherited nearly all his features from Lindsey, and nothing from Wayne except his sense of humor.

"Did you have to mow at the mink farm today?"

"Yes, why?"

I pointed to the piece of grass. He pulled out the strand, held it in his fingers, and blew, making a duck call.

"You're as sick as your old man," I said. That damn call brought me right back to the boat, and Will certainly knew it would.

"Oh no, he's got me beat on that score."

"How so?"

"After they got you in here yesterday, I went home and found him sitting at the kitchen table with a bottle and a shot glass."

Will said as soon as he sat down, Wayne hurled the saltshaker. It hit the backsplash above the sink and rolled onto the counter, stopping in front of the toaster. He took a box of cigarette papers out of his breast pocket, laid out a paper, sprinkled tobacco onto it and arranged the brown shreds with his fingers. He looked at Will, his skin turning red and his eyes narrowing. He rolled the sheet into a tube and brought it to his lips. "Fucking Jay and Percival, that spoiled little shit, I knew they would get into some kind of trouble." He spat on the paper and sealed the edges. The phone rang and Wayne picked up the receiver.

"Dad, how did they handle it?" Wayne asked.

"How do you think?" Grandpa yelled loud enough for Will to hear it come out of the phone. "Listen, we need to get the boat from the hospital dock, so no one goes snooping around."

"Why me? Fucking Lancelot and Percival should do it."

"It can't wait. Sheriff Edwards wants it done now and Lance won't get here for another couple hours."

"All right, then we better get to it."

Wayne put the papers and tobacco away and poured a finger of whiskey. Will said he tossed it back so fast it probably didn't touch the inside of his mouth.

They went out to the shed behind the house to collect tools. I had been over there many times with Dad to furl the nets after fishing season. The building smelled of mildew and tar from stored nets. Yellow oilskin suits with black stains hung from hooks on the back wall. Once inside, they sidled around the old tow truck used to spread nets after tarring. The close quarters made it difficult to move around and get anything done.

Wayne grabbed two suits, a galvanized metal bucket, a mop and a coil of garden hose, plus a handful of rags. He dropped it all in a fish box behind the cab of the truck. Wayne got in and told Will to open the doors to the shed.

The doors split in the middle and opened outward. Wayne backed out the truck. Will swung each door of the shed closed with a sweep of his arm. He climbed into the cab.

"I don't want to go back there."

"I don't care what you want. You were in charge of those two. Now you have to clean up the mess."

Wayne backed into the street. Will looked past the elms, the waterfront and the Number Two, to the lake. He said the waves rolled across the horizon as though they were sliding off the edge of the world.

Will choked up. He told me he couldn't figure out where he had failed. He'd learned to play hockey as his dad taught him; enrage the defenders to distraction through endless taunts and take advantage of their lapsed concentration. He did well in school—when he paid attention. Even though he was one of the better hockey players and girls loved his blue eyes, he wasn't popular. He avoided all school functions. I remember seeing on his bedroom wall a piece of paper with each number from one to one hundred and seventy written on it. One number for each school day. In some cases, the 'x' on a day's number went through to the wall.

"We'll tow it to the fishery and wash it on the slip," Wayne said.

Wayne parked in front of the fishery. Will carried the fish box to the slip. They pulled on the oilers and headed out in the fishing boat.

While Wayne made the turn from the fishery into the river, Vern stepped out the kitchen door of the Number Two. He set down a trash bin, smiled and waved, then extended his arms out with the palms up, questioning why they would be heading out. Wayne waved back and pointed to Will. Vern nodded, picked up the bin and went back inside.

At the hospital dock, the duck boat squeaked from rubbing against the piling. As they got closer, Will said the mess in the stern revealed itself.

"Jesus Christ. You boys really screwed the pooch this time."

Will sat in the back of the pilothouse under the rifle. Wayne motioned for him to take the helm.

"Keep us steady while I get the bow line. I'll tie it off on a stern cleat."

Will said the starboard side of the stern was covered in blood. It looked like someone pitched a gallon of red paint against the rear bench and the gunwale. There was a smeared handprint on top of the motor.

Wayne stepped onto the dock. He reached into the duck boat near the middle seat and lifted out the gun, holding it up in his left hand. With his right hand he took the duck boat's bow line and walked along the port side of the fishing boat. On the way back to the fishery, Will sat on an empty fish box in the bow, as far away from Wayne as possible.

At the fishery, Wayne pulled the duck boat by the bow line onto the slip and secured it.

"Will, hook up the hose."

Will stood on the landing, fixated on the duck boat, his feet anchored in place.

"Get moving. We need to get this done and the light's going."

Will shuffled toward the fishery dock. When he got there, a green Ford Maverick pulled up next to the old wrecker and honked. Two hockey teammates in letter jackets leaned out the windows. The one on the driver's side hollered, "Hey Will, you wanna go to the show tonight?"

Wayne shook his head.

"Can't. Have to help my dad." Will held up the hose.

The rear tires spit stones as they drove off.

"Do you think they saw anything?"

"No. They're thinking about who they can feel up tonight, not what's in front of them. Now let's get to work."

Will turned on the water and put the end of the hose over his shoulder. The tail dragged across the planks. Turning away, he walked to the end of the slip, picked up the mop and bucket, and set them next to the boat.

"What's going to happen?"

Wayne took the hose and squeezed the sprayer trigger to test the water pressure.

"I don't know. I expect we'll have to talk to the sheriff."

The spray drops splashed on the surface of the river beyond the stern.

"It wasn't my fault. It happened so fast, there was nothing I could do."

The water settled and resumed its flow to the lake. A small arrow of geese flew overhead, the brushing sound of their wings emerging from the splash of the last sprayer drops.

"You have to apologize to Aunt Julia. You were responsible for—"

"Dad, I didn't do anything!"

"That's right, goddamnit!"

Wayne jerked on the hose to provide slack and started spraying the bow so the water cascaded down the hull. As he swirled the nozzle underneath the forward bench, a light red mist rose over the stern. The wind carried the mist in a looping cloud away from the boat out over the river, where it evaporated.

"Why do I have to apologize?"

"You said it yourself. You didn't do anything. You were a spectator instead of keeping them out of trouble." Rust colored water and debris collected in the stern. "Hand me a rag." Wayne released the sprayer trigger and dropped the hose.

Will picked up the bucket. He pulled out a rag—the remains of a pajama top he recognized, blue with galloping brown horses, and handed it to Wayne, who ran it over the gunwale. "You know, this is how they taught us to polish belt buckles in the Air Force." The spray had not done its job in certain spots, so he knelt and scrubbed.

Wayne reached into the murky water below the motor to open the drain. The plug squealed and squeaked but wouldn't come out. His hand slipped and bilge water splashed his face. He wiped the sticky water away, creating dark brown smears below his eyes.

"Dump out the rags and hand me the bucket. Why did you run to Grandpa's house? Why didn't you go home?"

"You were at the ranch. We couldn't go to Uncle Pete's, and I know you wouldn't have wanted us to go to Aunt Mary's. There was nowhere else to go."

He dipped the bucket into the bilge water. Will sat in the grass at the top of the slip. He watched the channel marker beacons flash, nearly hypnotizing him. When Wayne could no longer dip the bucket, they tipped the boat on its side to dump the rest.

"Take them rags and finish wiping the inside," Wayne said.

Wayne walked to the truck. He pulled a cigarette from his breast pocket and twisted the ends. Will swabbed inside the hull, glancing up occasionally. Wayne looked down at him over the top of his smoke. As each rag grew damp and heavy, Will dropped it in the bucket. The wind mixed the clouds; they became thick and turned from gray to ash to black as the sun moved toward the horizon. Opening his thumb and index finger with a deliberate flourish, Wayne let the butt fall from his hand. He ground the cigarette into the gravel.

"I'm finished," Will said.

Wayne looked over the stern. They removed the motor and put it on the rack inside the fishery. They turned the boat keel up. Will carried the fish box with the tools back to the truck. The sun fell behind the trees on the south side of the river. Will stared out the windshield.

"What about Mom?"

"I'll tell her when we get home." Wayne turned the key and started the truck.

"What about the kids at school? What should I say?"

"You're just going to have to deal with it. Everyone in town will know soon enough. I'm sure it will be in next week's Pioneer."

"It wasn't my fault."

"Yes it was. It happened while you were in charge. Now, let's get home."

Will came over to the bed. "I can't believe it. He thinks I'm responsible for Percival shooting you."

"It's not your fault," I said. "Don't worry. I know whose fault it is, and it's not yours."

He thanked me and walked out; his posture worse than when he arrived.

Mom came in after her shift ended. She collapsed into the chair near the window, stretching her legs parallel to the floor. Dad came in behind her and walked straight over to me. He grabbed the bed rail.

"What the hell happened out there? Was Will daydreaming? How could he have let this happen?"

"Will came in this afternoon," I said.

"Did he apologize?" He glanced at Mom. "Did you see him? Did he apologize to you?" She shook her head.

"He doesn't need to apologize," I said. "It wasn't his fault."

Dad's boots rasped on the floor. He slid his hands back and forth on the railing and stared out the window.

"Did you piss your pants when they brought you in?" I said.

"Hell no!"

When he turned to face me, I knew he'd lied.

Sixteen: November 1976

Lying in the dark, I watched the shadows of tree branches wave on the walls. The hospital rumbled and groaned and breathed like a concrete monster. I thought of girls. I counted backward. Sheets of rain beat against the window. The night dragged by in a haze of half asleep and half awake. In the half-sleep, I found myself back in the boat, detached and spinning.

First light came in a gray, thin line, which grew into a rectangular beam. I didn't see the progression, even though it happened before my eyes. The rectangle contained black water spots that changed shape as the beam moved across the wall.

A click and the flash of lights jarred me awake. Mom leaned over the bedrail. "Hi, sweetheart. How did you sleep?"

"Awful." The air in my lungs rushed out. "Where's Dad?"

"It's Sunday. He's at home making pancakes for Robert and Dave. Are you hungry?"

"Not really."

"Sweetheart, Lance and Percival are on their way here. They're heading back to the Cities and need to leave soon."

"Do I have to see them?"

"It will be a long time before the next opportunity."

"So what?" I sank into the mattress. "Can you turn the lights off?"

"No. I think it would be good for you and Percival to talk. You can rest after they've gone."

"What about Dad?"

"Don't worry. We'll be with you while they're here."

Mom sat down in the chair near the window. A few minutes later, the doctor came in with another nurse. My skin stretched as the nurse removed the dressing. I fixed my gaze on Mom's face to distract myself from the pain. The doctor checked the tubes and said the closure was healing nicely. While the nurse applied a new dressing, Mom held my gaze. Once they'd finished with my arm, the nurse and the doctor huddled near the door. The doctor wrote notes on a clipboard. Mom joined them. I tried to follow their gestures but couldn't hear anything. After the huddle broke, Mom said she was going down to the lobby.

Lance guided Percival into the room by the shoulders. Mom and Dad followed them in. Percival's head tilted to the floor and his arms didn't move. He had on the plaid flannel shirt he'd worn when we went to the movie. Lance steered him away from the chair to the bedside.

"Hi," he said, half raising his hand. I barely heard him.

Lance took his hands off Percival. "We wanted to see you before we left." Lance nudged Percival. Percival's face twisted. His eyes narrowed, and his mouth slid to one side.

"I'm sorry," he said. Again barely audible. He squirmed. He looked up at Lance, who nodded his approval. "I slipped…and pulled the trigger." He grabbed the bedrail. "I couldn't help it. I slipped, and…it just went off, and–"

"I don't want to hear it."

"Just go," Dad said, with his arms crossed over his chest. "He's made his apology. Now get out of here."

"Let the boys talk," Lance said. "It will be good for them. They need to learn from this."

"That's funny! You don't think they've learned enough already?" Dad marched in front of Lance. "Well, how's this for a lesson? Your son is an uncoordinated klutz, and my son lost his arm because of it. Now he's–"

"Listen, maybe the lesson here is that you…" He pointed his finger in Dad's face, paused to look at Percival and me, then Mom. "No, you're going to have to figure this one out for yourself. Or maybe you have, and you refuse to accept it."

I pushed the water glass on the bedside table to the floor. "Get out! I can't stand this."

They slowly stepped out the door, except Percival, whose hands turned white with his grip on the bedrail.

"I'm not going. I'm not finished yet," Percival said.

Mom lingered in the doorway. "Sweetheart, is that okay?"

Percival stared down at me, his grip firm and eyes pleading.

"It's okay. I'll listen to what he has to say."

Mom stepped into the hall. The door clicked shut behind her.

"You always get me into trouble." Percival let go of the railing. "I'm sick of it! You get away with everything, and I end up with the blame." He walked in circles between the bed and the window waving his arms. "Your parents don't care what you do! Mine make me feel bad no matter what. I hate this! I hate having to apologize for things that aren't my fault."

I raised the bandaged stump of my right arm with all its attached drain tubes. "Does it look like I got away with *this*?" Pain fired through my shoulder into my chest. "I didn't force you to steal. Or throw candy at the movie."

"This isn't my fault, like all the other shit you've gotten me into." He stopped at the right side of the bed. "There's something wrong, and I can't figure out what, but I will. Someday I'm going to figure it out."

Lance poked his head in through the door. "Percival, we need to get going. I want to get home before it gets dark." The window bristled with leaves pushed by the wind.

"We're finished," I said.

Lance stepped into the room. Mom and Dad were not with him. He put his arm around Percival, and they left.

Seventeen: November 1976

Three afternoons a week, a nurse led me to an exercise room in the hospital basement. The first lesson, even before how to put on my new arm, was how to singlehandedly pull on a T-shirt. A strap around my chest with a bicycle cable at the end controlled the arm's movement. I wore the T-shirt to prevent the strap from chafing my skin. To move the strap and bend the arm at the elbow, I leaned forward or opened my shoulders. If I wanted to use the hand clamp, I locked the elbow and used the same motions. Each session, I learned a different task: how to put on the T-shirt and the arm itself, how to hold a knife and fork, how to put on my clothes, and how to tie my shoes. I spent the other afternoons learning how to write with my left hand and doing schoolwork brought in by my cousin Lizzie, Mary's daughter.

In mid-November, on my last day in the hospital, Mom came in with a white paper bag from Wings, the local clothing store. Dad waited down in the car. She pulled out a pair of blue boxer shorts from the bag. Until then I'd worn briefs, frustrated by the tangling and bunching. She laid them over the armrest of the guest chair. Next out of the bag was a stiff pair of jeans with the poster board label attached. Last out of the bag was a black-and-yellow Worland Warriors sweatshirt. She asked if I needed any help getting my clothes on. I told her I could do it, and she said she'd wait in the hall in case I needed help. I struggled to get the neckline of the sweatshirt past my overgrown hair. With the shirt half over my head, I asked her to come in. She tugged it down over my ears, kissing me on the forehead after the neckline fell into place.

Mom didn't say anything to Dad when she brought me out to the car. I got in the front seat, and she went right back to work.

Dad took me to the barbershop. Mom usually cut my hair in the kitchen. I'd sit on a cold metal stool while she scissored my hair into a ragged cut. The barber shop had two heavy chrome chairs with black leather seats. Old photos of Worland high school hockey players covered two walls. Ernie, the owner, a small man with barely a hair left on his head, napped in the second chair. The clang of the doorbell startled him awake.

"Ernie," Dad said.

"Pete, good to see you." He straightened his smock. "Want a touch-up?"

Dad pointed at me.

"It's about time you brought him in. Your old man was just here. He left about an hour ago."

"Is that right? How was he?" Dad said.

"Cranky. He couldn't stop talking about what's going on in St. Paul. I could hardly follow it." He smiled at me. "What are we doing for this young man today?"

"I—"

"High and tight, Ernie…and a shave."

"I don't want a buzzcut!"

"You can get whatever kind of haircut you want when *you* pay for it."

"Are you going to start paying me to work?"

"Ha! That's funny. Do you think Grandpa paid me when I was your age? You get three squares a day and a roof over your head. You're going to work where and when I say."

He grabbed my left arm and led me to the second chair. Ernie chuckled as he draped a white barber cape over my chest.

I sat with my back to the mirror. Two pictures of Wayne stared back from the wall: one an action shot in a Worland Warriors jersey with his arms up and the other a formal shot in a Gophers jersey. Dad sat across from me on a worn red couch beneath the photos. He picked up a *Playboy* magazine, put it down, and picked up a *Field & Stream*. Ernie ran the clipper over my scalp. Clumps of hair rolled off the cape onto the floor. It was over in a minute or two. Cold air chilled the back of my head.

"Do I have any hair left?"

Ernie tilted the seatback down. "You've got a lot more than me." He wrapped my face in a hot towel.

"How's business?" Ernie lapped a razor over a strop in a steady rhythm.

"Going to hell," Dad said. "I have to go to St. Paul with the old man in January. The state wants to shut us down. How about you?"

"That Hildegaard girl is opening a *salon* in the old bank building. She thinks men want their hair *styled*. Can you believe that?"

"Wayne will be the first one in there. He has hair to his shoulders now."

Ernie pulled the towel off and spread warm lather under my nose and around my jaw. I closed my eyes while he drew the blade over my cheeks and chin. He patted on aftershave that smelled like medicine.

"How does that feel?"

"It burns."

He pushed up the back of the chair. Dad put the magazine down and stared at me. Ernie ran the blade over the back of my neck in several quick strokes. "Done." He snapped off the barber's cape with a matador's flourish. "What do you think, boss?"

"Perfect," Dad said.

Ernie patted my shoulders. "The girls will love you." He spun the chair to face the mirror. My hand clamp banged on the metal armrest.

"They're not going to notice my hair."

"You'll get over it."

Dad dropped me off at home. He said he was going to mend nets with Grandpa, and I should come by the shed after I did my schoolwork. The hum of the refrigerator filled the empty house. Worksheets and folders from school lay strewn across my bed. I swept them onto the floor, lay down and went to sleep.

Two hours later, I walked the two blocks to the shed behind Wayne's house. I expected to find Dad and Grandpa sitting on the old wooden office chairs with a net heaped between them, weaving their net needles through sections of torn mesh. Instead, I found Grandpa alone, reclining with his eyes closed, listening to opera music that floated out of a console radio the size of my dresser. The fishing boat, with sanded patches and several hull staves missing, sat on a keel stand and poppets.

"Where's Dad?"

"He's at the mink farm." Grandpa didn't open his eyes. "He said you might turn up."

"What happened?"

"He wanted to listen to CCR. I have no idea who or what that is, but I didn't want to hear it."

"It's rock 'n' roll. He listens to it all the time. Mom likes it, too."

"Anyway, I told him to help Wayne get ready for pelting." He waved his arms at the net and the boat. "This stuff can wait."

The empty office chair squeaked and rattled as I rolled it across the dirt floor. I sat down next to him.

"That's quite a haircut," he chuckled. "Did you join the Marines?"

"It was Dad's idea. I hate it."

"The girls will love it. You're not shaggy like everyone else."

"I bet. They're all gonna fight to dance with the one-armed boy." I spun in the chair, holding up my new arm.

He grabbed the back of the chair. "Knock it off. Be grateful you're alive." His eyes turned icy. "Your mother married a man with one leg. Now sit still for a minute. Listen."

"What is this music?" The sound floated on the crackling of the fire in the wood stove.

"It's from an opera called Pagliacci. It's about a clown."

"He's laughing but doesn't sound very happy."

"He's not. His wife has gone off with another man and he's laughing at his own pain. He hopes it will reduce his suffering and turn it into a joke."

"Where did you learn about opera?"

"At college. I had to take a humanities course: painting, architecture, classical music, literature. Opera sounded like shrieking at first. Once I understood it, other music sounded small. I went to operas for class and kept going after it ended. You might learn a thing a two from Canio—that's the clown's name."

"Like what?"

"Laugh at your misfortune. Your dad has never been able to do that. He's beaten himself up for almost twenty years. Now he's going to beat himself up over what happened to you. He doesn't have Wayne's devil-may-care attitude."

"Why didn't you and Grandma come see me in the hospital?"

"We had to go to the Cities to see specialists for Grandma. Also, us hanging around there would have made your dad feel worse. I think he blames himself but won't admit it."

"Maybe he's right. Maybe he should blame himself."

"What good does that do, making himself miserable over something he can't change?"

"Maybe he should be miserable."

"Why?"

"Because I am. He should have gone with us instead of Will, and he lied to me."

"About what?"

"He said he didn't pee in his pants on the way to the hospital."

"Why does it matter?"

"Because I admitted it, and he wouldn't."

"I honestly don't know if he did or didn't. Jim and Moose worked fast to keep him alive— and by the way, you wouldn't be here if it weren't for them. His pants were soaked with blood and water from lying on the deck. We barely got him to the plane at Buffalo Point. Swede didn't think he'd make it."

"What's wrong with Grandma?"

"She has a glioblastoma. That's brain cancer."

"Can they cure it?"

"I don't know. That's why we've been going to the Cities, to see what can be done. Speaking of what can be done, what are you going to do? What do you want?"

"I want my arm back. I wanted to become a fisherman like Dad… and like you. Now I don't know what to do."

"I wanted to become an engineer and ended up a fisherman and mink farmer. Listen Jay, another thing I studied in college is philosophy, and I believe that it's not what happens to you but how you react to it. You'll be all right if you don't let this dictate your life. Your dad and Wayne never moved on from their injuries. I gave them the same speech I just gave you and they didn't listen." He looked at me with watery eyes and pulled a red handkerchief from his back pocket before wiping his nose. "I tell you what, I have a deal for you."

"What is it?"

"I'll keep your dad busy at the mink ranch for the winter," he waved again at the dismantled boat and heap of damaged nets, "if you help me deal with the mess in here."

"Why should I?"

"Do you want to move on from this or not?"

"I want to get my own haircuts."

"All right then, I'll pay you, but there's three conditions."

"What are they?"

"First, if I ask you to do something, you do it, and I don't want to hear any complaints. Second, you listen and acknowledge what I say. Remember, there's a reason you have two ears and one mouth, you get me?"

I nodded. He stared at me, waiting.

"Yes, I get it."

"Good. The last, and most important, is that you can't spend any of the money until you graduate from high school."

"That's three years! Why?"

"You have to trust me." He stood up and held out his right hand for me to shake.

I stared at it, not knowing what to do. "What about haircuts?"

"Get a hat."

I grabbed his hand with my left and shook it.

"Good. Come back tomorrow after school and we'll get started."

Over the course of that first winter, Grandpa taught me all the skills required to maintain the boat: how to use the steam box and bend wood, how to replace hull staves, how to replace a rib, how to apply epoxy, how to remove and disassemble the engine, and how to maintain the prop and the rudder. For Christmas, Grandpa and Grandma gave me a black wool hat.

As spring approached, he taught me how to use a net needle to make and repair nets. Each afternoon started with him asking how school went, and how much homework I had to do. If I had any, we started with that, and I had to finish it with his approval before we worked on the boat. On some afternoons we never got to the boat work after I struggled with a geometry proof or a history paper.

We launched the repaired boat on a cold April morning. Wayne drove the farm truck with the boat trailer to the shed. Dad and Grandpa lifted her off the poppets using a block and tackle around each end. I pulled out the poppets, and they lowered her onto the trailer. We launched her from the fishery slip. As she slid down the ways into the water, Wayne poked my shoulder with his index finger.

"I hope she still floats."

"I bet she stays afloat longer than you."

"Jay," Grandpa hollered from on deck, "you're the pilot. Let's take her out for a shakedown."

I piloted the boat out into the river and onto the open lake. She performed flawlessly that day, and that summer—the engine's power steady, the helm responsive and the hull watertight. We spent days with sixteen hours of sunlight hauling nets from six in the morning until two in the afternoon. I worked alongside Dad and my brother Robert, while Grandpa watched from beneath a long-billed cap. It took most of the summer for me to learn how to move my arm through the various positions required to reach over the side, grab the net and pull it over the gunwale. In midsummer, I fashioned a chamois chest protector to stop the arm strap from abrading my skin. By the end of summer, I was moving 50-pound fish boxes around the boat like chess pieces.

That fall, ice severely damaged the nets. Ten of eighteen had to be remade over the winter. The boat required routine engine maintenance and minor hull repair. One day after we'd finished the day's mending, I asked Grandpa how he built the boat.

"I used a half-hull model at 1:18 scale."

He walked to the bench at the back of the shed and reached into the rafters. Though I'd worked in the shed for nearly two years, I'd never noticed the model fixed to a crossbeam.

"How did you make it?"

"I started with a design drawing." He pulled a long, rolled-up piece of paper from a workbench drawer. "This is a blueprint, a copy made from my original drawing." He unrolled the paper and anchored one end with a hammer and the other with a wrench. "I used a print like this to make templates. The drawing shows lifts, or sections, of the hull, and profile guides. I cut out the sections and glued them to a poster board. I cut the sections from the poster board and used them as templates to trace the shape of each section on a three-quarter by four mahogany board."

"Can we make one?" I looked at the drawing, unable to imagine how he turned five rectangular pieces of wood into the graceful lines of the fishing boat.

"When Lance was about your age, I showed him how to do it. His model is over the doors." He pointed to the double doors at the end of the shed. It was mounted above the center of the door frame. Brown dust covered it to the extent that it nearly matched the timber behind it. Once he pointed it out, I noticed all kinds of other items hanging from the joists or nailed to the walls: a helm, oily motor parts, a string of net floats, a tattered pennant, a pair of torn oiler pants, and a cracked and dry work boot.

"Did my dad make one?"

"No, he never showed any interest."

"What about Wayne?"

"Ha! He started and never finished. You know who made a beautiful model? Mary. It's over my desk at the house. Nobody notices it because of her paintings, or they think it's the one I made. The real ones get beat up as they're used to build the boat. That's why the finish on this one is worn off and the sections are loose." He handed the model to me.

I held it with my clamp and ran my left hand over the surface. It felt smooth and true, even with the visible damage.

"Why do you have all that broken stuff on the walls? Why not throw it away?"

"They're memories, reminders. Some good. Some bad."

"Are the pants and the boot what I think they are?"

"No one *really* knows what another person thinks." He tapped the side of his head with his index finger. "We're all stuck in here by ourselves."

My model took two weeks to build, between net mending and homework. I cut the wood using the band saw at the mink farm. Wayne had a good laugh as I cut well outside the lines to make sure I had enough excess material.

"Well, at least you can't cut off any fingers."

"Well, at least I'm going to finish the job."

"What's the point? You'll never build a boat."

"I want to see if I can do it."

"I know what you're thinking, and you're wasting your time."

"You have no idea what I'm thinking." I tapped the side of my head.

"Gave you the philosophy speech, did he? Be careful, that stuff can drive you mad."

Back at the shed, I nailed the lifts together in haste, switching the bottom two so I had to pry the whole thing apart and reassemble it. I spent another next week chiseling and sanding the surface into shape, using the profile guides from the drawing to verify the contour. After ten days of applying lacquer and sanding it down, and a year after I lost my arm, I handed the finished model to Grandpa.

"You did a fine job. Where do you plan to hang it?"

"I don't know. I haven't thought about that."

"That's good. Better to think about the process than the result. If you don't mind, I'd like to hang it up in here, over the workbench."

"Actually, I know where I'd like it to go." I took two nails from a rusty coffee can on the workbench and grabbed the hammer. "I want to put it here, over the boot."

I brought over the stepladder and climbed to the third rung. Grandpa handed me a tape measure. I marked the nail locations. With each swing of the hammer, I drove the nail true to the wall without a single miss. I'd done what Dad couldn't or wouldn't do. I stepped down to the dirt floor, like an astronaut stepping off the lunar lander onto the surface of the moon.

"What do you want to do next?"

"I want to build a house."

"That's a big project. I built the one your dad grew up in from a Sears Roebuck kit."

"I mean a model of a house."

"Sounds like you might want to be an architect, if you like to build models."

"I guess so, if that's what architects do."

"Making models is one thing architects do, but to design a good model, whether it's a boat or a building, you need to study math, engineering and art. Building the model is the easy part. If you're serious about it, you have to go to college, maybe serve an apprenticeship, and if you're ambitious, build your own practice."

I sank with the impossibility of it. Worlands went to college. Brennans worked with their backs, not with their brains. To me, Grandpa and Lance had gone to a faraway land called "college." One barely survived the journey, and the other never returned.

"Look, spring is almost here. School will be over soon. Let's finish mending these nets. How about we take up building that house in the fall?"

That summer Dad, my brothers, and I fished. Dad didn't say much other than to bark out commands or curse the "college educated, pinheaded politicians" in St. Paul. Grandpa came out occasionally, but he mostly stayed at home to be with Grandma. Her cancer had advanced to the point where she couldn't speak. When I'd remind Dad that Mom went to college, he'd call me a smart-ass and say that maybe I belonged with educated pinheads, before tossing back another four of the aspirin he now constantly chewed.

On a rainy October day, Grandpa lowered a drawing table he'd mounted with hinges to the shed wall. Behind the table, on a small shelf, sat a metal box with a leather-bound case inside. He opened the case to reveal a set of tools, mounted in green velvet, that resembled surgical instruments.

"I used these tools to make the boat drawing. They're the same tools an architect would use to design a house." He laid each tool on the table and explained its purpose. From a shelf above the workbench, he pulled down a thick green book with a beat-up cover. "This is the mechanical drawing textbook I used in college. You need to go through the first half of this book and practice before you design your dream house, and you need to finish your regular schoolwork each day before we do anything in here." He rapped the drawing book with his knuckles. "I imagine that will take until New Year's. And, we need to fill out your application for the U."

"I don't think Dad wants me to do that."

"Don't worry, your mother and I will deal with him."

Eighteen: February 1981

I came home from school and found Dad sitting at the kitchen table with an envelope in his hand. He'd just returned from a week in St. Paul with Grandpa. He tapped the envelope on the Formica tabletop. The upper left corner of the envelope had the gold "M" of the University of Minnesota. The house groaned from the late-February wind and snow pounding it.

"How was St. Paul?"

"Who put you up to this?" He waved the envelope and dropped it on the table.

"No one."

"Really. You did this all by yourself."

"I had help."

"Is that right?" He squinted at me and clenched his jaw. "Is that what you and Grandpa did all that time in the shed?" I imagined a bomb ticking underneath the table.

"No, we repaired the nets and the boat, and I'm working on a house model. Besides, they may not have accepted me."

He slid the envelope across the table. I didn't want to open it. I enjoyed the tension of not knowing. No matter the outcome, I had the sense it would deflate me, my future decided rather than a sense of possibility. I put my finger below the flap.

"Don't do that. You might tear something important." Dad slid his pocketknife across the table.

I pulled out the main blade and ran it under the fold. Inside were papers of various colors, and a cover letter on embossed stationery. I read the first line out loud.

"Congratulations on your admission to the University of Minnesota College of Design, School of Architecture, for Fall Quarter 1981."

"Goddamnit! You two really did it! Without consulting me or your mother!"

My hand shook as I slid the cover letter back across the table. "Mom knows."

He picked it up, and began read it over. "Christ! We can't afford to send you to college in the Cities. She knows that! We don't have the damn money, and I need your help, particularly after what happened in St. Paul." He set the paper down. "Look, it's simple. You're not going. That's all there is to it."

"I'm going, with or without your help."

"We'll see about that."

"What happened in St. Paul?"

"I'm tired. I'll let your grandpa tell you about it." He gave the letter a final glance and tossed it toward me. "You listen to him more than me." He got up, went into the bedroom and closed the door.

I found Grandpa as I did that first day home from the hospital, reclining, with his eyes closed, conducting *Nessun dorma*, one of his favorite arias, with a net needle. I held up the envelope. "I'm in!"

"Vinceró!" He tossed the needle into the rafters.

"Dad was not happy."

He stood up. "Let me see the letter." I handed him the envelope. "Does your mother know you got in?"

The needle had landed on my recently started house model and collapsed a section of the frame. I picked it out of the debris. "No, Dad was sitting there with it when I got home from school." I told him how Dad had reacted.

"He's had a tough week."

"What happened in St. Paul? Is it that bad?"

"It is — for him."

"What about you?"

"I'm an old man, Jay. Listening to opera is as close to passionate as I get these days, especially after this trip." He sat back down. "Do you want to hear what went on down there?"

"I do."

Dad and Grandpa arrived just in time for their four o'clock meeting with Senator Carlson, who represented Worland in the Minnesota Senate. The Capitol building was vibrant. Hordes of well-dressed staffers rushed from one office to another in preparation for the legislative session. They were in the flannel shirts and jeans they'd worn on the drive down, and the quickly moving bureaucrats watched them as if they were alien invaders.

The door to Carlson's office suite had his name stenciled on the glass, along with a small Worland Windows logo in the lower right corner. A secretary greeted them in the anteroom and told them to go right in. Senator Carlson was on the phone, leaning on the edge of his desk, one leg dangling and the other on the ground. He waved them in and pointed to the chairs in front of his desk. Rather than end the call, Carlson continued talking while they sat down. There must have been something he wanted them to hear, because good politicians don't do anything without considering all the angles.

"Yes, but I don't care what the editor at the Tribune says about gambling. I need you to start counting heads for the Indian Bingo bill. Understand?" His eyes fixed on the ceiling while he listened. "Okay. Goodbye."

As Carlson hung up the phone, his shoulders loosened. He strode around the desk and sat down, stretching his arms over the blotter.

"Arthur, Pete. How was the drive?"

Dad broke his day-long silence. "It was fine." He'd tossed back aspirin every two hours during the trip. Grandpa had the sense Dad wanted a fight to relieve his tension. "Are we getting a bingo parlor in Worland?"

"We have to legalize them first." Carlson dripped coyness. "Where they'd put them is anybody's guess."

"You're full of shit. I don't know how you live with yourself." Dad started to get up out of his chair. "And who the hell's going to come to Worland to play bingo?" Grandpa put his arm in front of Dad. Carlson grabbed the sides of his chair, his condescension sliding toward anger after such a direct confrontation of his cleverness. Nothing is more sacred to a politician than his ego, and bruising Carlson's would not help. Grandpa needed to get the conversation under control.

"Senator, I'm sorry. My son is new to the legislative process." Dad settled into his seat. Grandpa hated to push him back into silence, but he saw no other way to handle the situation. "As you know, we're here to talk about commercial fishing on Lake of the Woods, not bingo."

"We are indeed." Carlson straightened his tie. "Listen, I've seen the DNR's assessment, and I'm sure you have too. Although it says the lake is healthy and commercial fishing does no harm, the public's perception is otherwise."

Dad lurched forward in his chair. "And how did that happen?"

Grandpa put his arm out again. "Senator, please go on."

"Well, the resort owners and sportsmen's groups have invested in advertising and newspaper coverage. In the public's mind, particularly here in the Cities, commercial fishing takes away from sport fishing. They want Lake of the Woods closed to commercial fishing, and I'm here to serve the public interest."

"Well, I'm the public too—and I have an interest." Grandpa stood up, putting his hands on the front edge of the desk. "I want to speak at the Senate Game and Fish committee hearing tomorrow. Put me on the testifier list. Maybe the committee will listen to reason."

"I'm sure they will." Carlson grinned and leaned back in his chair. "I'll add you to the list."

They arrived at the committee room at a quarter to nine, fifteen minutes before the hearing was to begin. The last time Grandpa had seen Pete in a suit was at Grandma's funeral. Senator Carlson, the committee chairman, sat at the center of the dais. When he spotted them, he sent over an aide, who told Grandpa he would speak last, which Grandpa thought would put him at a disadvantage. As the morning went on, the sportsmen and resort owners gave their usual speeches about fathers and sons fishing together, and how important family resorts were to the Lake of the Woods economy. The committee members began to fidget in their seats and pass notes to their assistants.

The last person to speak before Grandpa was Game and Fish Director Don Doscaras. Grandpa said that since they'd started fighting over fishing regulations, Doscaras' hair had turned gray, and his had fallen out. The trawler defeat had forced Doscaras to return to an academic approach to game and fish management. One thing that hadn't changed was his ability to tranquilize an audience.

"Mr. Chairman, the two-year study by the University of Minnesota as part of the 1978 Lake of the Woods Commissioner's Order indicates commercial fishing has had no effect on the lake's sport fish population. During the study period, the number of commercial fishing operations declined from six to three, but the total catch weight remained constant. Despite the anecdotal evidence given in previous testimony, there has been no statistically significant change in the fish population. As Game and Fish Director, it is my opinion, based on the data, that commercial fishing should be allowed to continue, unless alternate forms of revenue to support the DNR's mission on Lake of the Woods are found to replace commercial license fees. And now, I'd be happy to answer questions."

Doscaras had buried the lede. He cared about facts, but he cared more about money. Carlson asked each man on the committee if they had any questions, and only Senator Lewis of Gopher Prairie responded.

"Mr. Doscaras, how much revenue per year will the state lose by eliminating commercial fishing licenses on Lake of the Woods?"

"About a thousand dollars, sir. The fee is forty-five dollars per pound net." Doscaras didn't flinch or look at his notes.

"And how many sport fishing licenses are issued by the state each year, and how much revenue do they generate?"

He answered without hesitation. "About one million two hundred thousand licenses, and seven and a half million dollars in revenue. The cost of an in-state sport license is six dollars and fifty cents."

"Thank you, Mr. Doscaras."

Senator Carlson called Grandpa to the podium. He couldn't figure out if Carlson had planted the question or if Lewis had acted on his own. While the official subject of the hearing was Carlson's Lake of the Woods commercial fishing bill, he now saw that the real subject was money for the DNR. To compete, Grandpa would need to appeal to their sense of integrity and fair play.

"Good morning, Mr. Chairman and committee members. Thank you for allowing me to testify today. My name is Arthur Brennan. My family has been fishing on Lake of the Woods for ninety years. In all that time, we have been able to count on the honest consideration of this body, until today. Four years ago, the sportsmen, resort owners, and fishing industry agreed to restrict commercial fishing access to certain areas of the lake in exchange for allowing the industry to continue. Today, the committee is considering reneging on that promise."

The members at the far ends of the dais began to whisper among themselves. *Reneged* is not a word any politician wants to see after their name in the paper. Grandpa had their attention.

"It is doing so without shame and based on anecdotal evidence from cherry-picked anglers and the groups they represent, while ignoring independent analysis that indicates the industry can continue with little or no impact." The whisperers stopped. "Passing Senator Carlson's ban will not only destroy the fishing and mink ranching businesses near Lake of the Woods, but it will also destroy the families it supports, as well as the credibility of this committee, and the state government. Furthermore—"

"Motion to adjourn," came from one end of the dais.

"Seconded," from the other.

Senator Carlson picked up the gavel and slammed it.

"This hearing is adjourned."

The members stood up and started to leave the room. That was when Grandpa knew. He walked back and sat next to Dad, who was looking at his feet, watching his right foot kick his left.

"So, what now?" Dad asked. "They didn't vote. They only asked about money and licenses, and nothing about fishing. I don't think they cared what was said."

"Welcome to the Capitol, Pete."

Senator Carlson's aide walked over to them. "The senator recommends that you spend the afternoon meeting with individual members of the committee. He's asked them to make time to see you, so that your concerns can be discussed in private."

Dad stood up and looked the assistant square in the face. "Why should we? Your boss is gearing up to vote us out of existence no matter what we do. It's his bill for Christ's sake."

Grandpa turned Dad by the shoulder and told the young man they'd make the rounds. After he went away, Grandpa faced Dad. "They don't want to talk about taking back promises and putting us out of business in a public hearing. What they say and do goes into the public record and is reported in the papers. This is our chance to negotiate."

"Negotiate what? They're going to pass the ban—"

"We still have a chance. If they try to take away our licenses with nothing in return, like when they took gill netting from the Indians on the Angle, they'll look like the liars and cheats they are. But if they give us something, they can look like considerate public servants."

In the afternoon, they joined the rushing hordes, meeting with one senator after another. The suburban senators treated them like a novelty. Some had to be shown Worland and Lake of the Woods on the state map hanging in their office. Others asked if they could get a good deal on a mink coat. An early sunset darkened the windows as they arrived at Senator Carlson's office. His secretary was gone, and the senator was sitting at his desk with the knot of his tie loosened.

"How did it go?" he asked, like a professor inquiring about the difficulty of a test.

"We want five more years."

Carlson guffawed. "And what does the state and the DNR get in return?"

"You avoid the appearance of giving us the same treatment as the Indians on the Angle."

"Not good enough. Everyone thinks we're crooks anyway. That won't change anyone's mind. What's in it for the state? What's in it for me? I want something tangible."

"Do you want to be remembered as the senator who took Minnesota Walleye off the menu of the world's restaurants?"

"Of course not, but that doesn't help me either."

"Can you arrange a meeting with Commissioner Rinke tomorrow? I think there is something we can do."

"And what might that be?"

"Give you a chance to do the right thing and get some positive press for yourself. Plus, generate additional revenue for the state."

He picked up a pen and a notepad from the desk. "Now you're speaking my language." He scrawled a note and stuck it on the phone receiver. "I'll have my assistant set it up first thing in the morning."

Grandpa had a miserable night's sleep. The nightcap at the hotel bar hadn't helped. He wanted company, someone who remembered things he remembered, someone who would go to Ireland with him, but he couldn't imagine another woman in the house. On the other hand, sitting home alone started to feel stupid rather than faithful. Round and round he went until he found himself waiting for the alarm to ring at seven.

Dad didn't appear to have gotten a good night's rest either. "I hate wearing a goddamn suit" was the first thing he said when he sat down for breakfast in the hotel restaurant. He barked at the waiter about the runny eggs and he bitched to Grandpa his bewilderment at politicians and the secret language they spoke, a language that never meant what it seemed to mean, but instead was apparently just a cover for what was really going on.

Grandpa told him politicians were not that complicated. He needed to forget about the issues and focus on money and their egos. They would have to offer revenue to the state and good press for Carlson to survive. By the time his re-cooked eggs came back, Dad had returned to silence.

Rinke and Doscaras were waiting for them at the conference table in the commissioner's office when they arrived at ten. Rinke greeted them.

"Good morning. How'd you sleep last night?"

"Fine," they said simultaneously. Grandpa was sure the dark circles under their eyes gave them away.

"Senator Carlson mentioned you have a response to his bill that might interest us." Rinke's eyes were clear. "After all, I see no reason why the state should put you out of business, given the results of the study."

They had an opening. Grandpa pulled out a notecard on which he had done some calculations. "Mr. Rinke, I believe it would be fair to allow license fees to increase with inflation."

"We do need more revenue to support enforcement and resource monitoring." Rinke fiddled with the handle of his mug.

Dad loosened his shirt collar. "In other words, you want a bigger cut of the business."

"Mr. Brennan, we're not the mafia." Rinke folded his hands and smiled.

"I'm having trouble seeing the difference." Dad's voice got higher as he spoke.

Rinke adopted a fatherly demeanor. "We have to pay scientists and game wardens a decent wage, as well as provide reliable equipment, in order to protect natural resources like Lake of the Woods."

"The Indians managed to survive for thousands of years without your help." The volume of Dad's voice increased. He shifted his leg, and it banged into one of the table supports. Grandpa put his arm in front of Dad.

"Would indexing the license fee to inflation meet the department's needs?"

"Yes," Doscaras joined in. "as long as you agree to a one-time base fee increase to one hundred dollars per net, so the initial license fee reflects fair market value."

"Done." Grandpa thought they had reached an agreement.

"Of course, that's contingent on Senator Carlson withdrawing his bill." Rinke took a long pull from his coffee. "However, without the support of the DNR or the governor, it'll be hard to pass. The suburban senators tend to follow our recommendations."

"Will you be speaking with the governor about it soon?"

"I have a meeting with him this afternoon, and I'll bring it up. I'll also speak with Senator Carlson. Come back tomorrow morning at nine and I'll let you know where we stand."

They went to Mickey's Diner for lunch. Dad picked a booth in the back corner, where a window overlooked the parking lot and no other patrons sat nearby. At the counter, tendrils of cigarette smoke mixed with coffee vapor to form a languorous haze.

A waitress placed two glasses of water on the table. Dad ordered toast with peanut butter, and a pot of coffee. Grandpa ordered a roast beef sandwich and apple pie.

"You're not hungry?"

"Not really."

They watched a young couple steadying each other on the icy sidewalk. "Those two look like they're in for a hard life." The couple disappeared around the corner.

Dad spun his knife on the tabletop.

"Pete, you need to think about your life. Mine's nearly over. In the long run, if the state decides they want to shut us down, they will, and you have to be prepared for that."

"What are you talking about? If we get five more years now, I can get five more when the time comes." Grandpa hadn't seen confidence from Dad in a long time, and he said it was good to see, no matter how misplaced. The thought of snuffing it out sent a stabbing sensation through his chest.

"I don't think so. With the animal rights groups fighting the mink business and the state fighting the fishing business, we're losing our power. I think we should ask the state for a buyout, while we have something to bargain with."

Dad pounded the end of his knife on the table. "How could you consider a buyout, let alone offer one up?" The chatter of the patrons around them stopped for a moment, then resumed.

"The way I see it, as time goes on, our position will only get worse."

"Dad, the lake and fishing are our life. Everything we have comes from the lake."

Grandpa wanted an *uisce beatha* more than a coffee.

"Pete, you need to think about your kids. Maybe if you get a chunk of money, you can help Jay go to college. He wants to become an architect."

"What happens to Julia and me? I'm forty years old. I have a long way to go. It's bad enough Julia is a nurse building windows at six dollars an hour for the Worlands. What am I gonna do?"

"You could become a fishing guide or take people out to the islands. Use some of the buyout money to start a new business. The work wouldn't be nearly as hard."

"I don't want to haul people from the Cities around the lake." He popped four aspirin into his mouth and gulped down half his water. "I want to keep fishing."

"I understand you're upset. This is not how I wanted things to go." Grandpa took his pipe out of his suit coat and filled it. "I'm trying to prepare you for when I'm gone." Dad reached across the table with his lighter and held it over the bowl while Grandpa inhaled, then lit the roll-your-own he took from his inside jacket pocket.

The waitress returned to the table with their coffee.

"You're going to have to put those out, you're in the no-smoking section." She gazed down at them, holding the coffee cups in one hand and the pot in the other. "Sir, it's state law."

Dad turned his eyes up at her. Grandpa could see the boil rising behind them. "Jesus fucking Christ." Dad crushed his cigarette out on the tabletop. "I don't believe this. The state says I can't have a coffee and a smoke with my dad?"

"You can, you just can't do it here." The waitress tilted her head toward Grandpa.

Grandpa used his pocketknife to scrape the embers from his pipe onto Pete's cigarette butt.

"Thank you." She put the cups on the table. "Would either of you like cream or sugar?"

Dad swept the butt and ashes off the table and onto the floor. "No, we take it black."

They were in the commissioner's office the next morning at nine, sitting at the conference table. The secretary brought in coffee and a box of donuts. After she left the room and closed the door, Rinke opened the cardboard box, smiled and offered them first pick. Dad took a jelly-filled and Grandpa took a chocolate glazed. Rinke took a maple-covered. Doscaras declined.

"What do you have for us?" Grandpa asked. "How did the meetings with the governor and Carlson go?"

Rinke looked at Doscaras and nodded. Doscaras watched them eat their donuts, obviously wanting one but denying himself.

"Senator Carlson and I have agreed to phase out commercial fishing on Lake of the Woods. To replace the lost revenue from commercial fishing licenses, Carlson and the sportsmen have agreed to a two-dollar increase in the annual sport license fee."

"This is bullshit." Dad's mouth was full, and he waved his donut. "We sat right here yesterday and agreed on a license fee increase—what happened?"

"Mr. Brennan, we had to sharpen our pencils and consider all the options." Rinke referred to a legal pad on the table in front of him. "The new sport license fees will provide a revenue increase of two million dollars a year. As part of the phaseout, the remaining commercial license holders can sell their licenses back to the state for eighty thousand dollars or fish for eight more years—until the 1990 season. For each year closer to 1990, the buyout declines by ten thousand dollars. At the close of the 1990 season, commercial fishing on Lake of the Woods will end."

Grandpa put down his donut. "There's no way it will pass. The governor has said he won't support closing the commercial fishery. Hell, the North Shore guys got nothing when the state shut them down. Why do you think their representatives will support a buyout for us?"

"They won't, but we have enough votes from southern and western Minnesota, plus the Cities, to pass it."

"What about the governor?"

"He's the one who suggested the phaseout, to make the transition as smooth as possible for the affected families."

Dad stood up, his body off balance due to the odd angle of his leg, and hurled his half-eaten donut against the wall, where it stuck on the map north of Mille Lacs, then slid down over St. Paul, leaving a raspberry trail in its wake. He pointed at Rinke first and then at Doscaras.

"Fuck you. And fuck you. I'm fishing until the last goddamn day."

I didn't know what Rinke would do," Grandpa said to me that February afternoon. "I wasn't sure if he'd call in troopers to remove us or simply walk out." He paused. "I had no choice. I said I'd transfer half the licenses to your dad and sell the rest back to the state."

I looked at him, waiting, suspecting.

"Anyway, after I said what I was going to do, Rinke walked out. Pete hardly said a word on the drive back." Grandpa picked up the letter and looked it over again. "You're going." He handed the letter and the envelope back to me. "Your mother will be thrilled. I am too."

I collected the papers and put them back in the envelope, knowing there was nothing left for me in Worland.

Nineteen: November 1986

Mary and Eddie had Thanksgiving at their new home, which was the old Calvin Worland house overlooking the river. The old man left it to them, and they spent two years and who knows how much money renovating the place. When Mary invited me, she said having everyone over for the holiday would make a great housewarming. I thought it might be more like a house fire.

At Grandma's funeral, Lance and his family had kept their distance. They arrived in the evening for the wake and left immediately after the funeral, saying nothing beyond cursory greetings and inquiries. I hadn't seen them since.

Mary conceded, after I pressed her, that she'd had to work to convince Eddie to invite the Brennan side of the family. He had good reason to think the old wounds might open — just talking about a gathering made me uncomfortable. Lance put up a lot of resistance and finally agreed to make the trip after Mary told him Grandpa wanted to personally congratulate Percival for graduating from Dartmouth. I had another year to finish my architecture degree. If Percival could find it within himself to come, I could do the same. Maybe something good would come from it.

Mary started Thanksgiving Day full of energy. I got there at the same time as Wayne, Lindsey, and Will. "I'm so glad you're here," Mary said. Will walked through the entry without pausing to say hello. Mary leaned toward me and spoke in a low voice. "Everyone's in the dining room. No trouble yet." She hugged Wayne. "What's in the box?"

"Something for Jay." I could hear Dad and Grandpa's voices from the other side of the house. Wayne unbuttoned his jacket. "Where's the beer?"

Lindsey slapped his backside. "We don't have our coats off yet."

"Honey, I think we should take the edge off before we go in there."

She kissed his cheek. "You're terrible. I can't go anywhere with you."

Lizzie and Daniel, Mary's two oldest, came to take our coats and the box. Lindsey pushed her hair behind her ears.

"When do we get a tour? I'm excited to see what you've done."

Mary extended her right arm. "We'll start in the kitchen—where the beer is."

Eddie presided over a six-burner range with bubbling pots. In the center of the room was an aircraft-carrier-sized island covered with discarded bowls and utensils. I asked him why he decided to take up cooking.

"I like to cook to blow off steam." He paused for effect, then turned serious. "I had an industrial engineering professor at the U tell me I could learn everything I needed to know about manufacturing in a kitchen, so I tried cooking. He was right, and I liked it."

Wayne took a bottle of beer from an ice-filled tub on the breakfast table. "Sounds like he taught you everything except how to actually build something."

Eddie raised a wooden spoon like he was about to hit him with it and smiled. "You always have the right line, don't you."

"Some of the professors I had at the school of hard knocks were as good as the ones I had at the U." Wayne used an opener hanging off the tub to remove the bottlecap. "Trust me, I've studied at both places." He flicked the cap over the island into the trash bin on the other side. "Let's start the tour. Mary, lead the way."

To call Mary and Eddie's place a mansion implies a grandeur it didn't have, but *house* is too puny a word. The decoration was deliberately modest, designed to promote their self-image as regular folks. The only exceptions were strategically placed paintings of the kind I had only seen in museums in the Cities, interspersed with Mary's scenes of people at work around Worland. The effort to appear ordinary failed, thanks to the sweeping vistas and staged furniture. The kids' bedrooms on the second floor were spacious. One had an expansive view of the front lawn, including a magnificent oak tree near the street and the tops of the nearby houses. At the end of the tour, Mary left us in the dining room, where the heavy table and numerous place settings reminded me of a medieval feast.

Lance and Gwen stood by the floor-to-ceiling windows, watching half a dozen geese paddle around a hole of open water in the otherwise frozen river. On the opposite side of the room, Mom and Dad sat talking underneath a painting of Grandpa bending down to move a fish box. I decided to talk to Lance first and get it out of the way. Wayne followed me. Lindsey excused herself to go see Mom and Dad.

"Lance, how are things in the Cities?" Wayne hugged him, and kissed Gwen on the cheek.

"Busy. We finished moving Percival back from New Hampshire last month. The fall colors were awesome." He stopped for a moment, as if his mind had briefly stopped working. "I hate that word—awesome—and now Percival's got me using it. Anyway, he spent the summer in New England goofing off, and now he's looking for a 'real job,' as he calls it." Lance chuckled.

"He's hoping he can find something out east." It sounded more like Gwen's wish than Percival's. "A lot of companies in Boston hire Thayer graduates."

Lance sipped his wine. "How are you doing? How are things at the ranch?" Lance's growing resemblance to Grandpa, minus the lightly held wine glass, unnerved me. Grandpa always held his tumbler of whiskey with a firm grip, as he was doing now, talking with my brother Robert at the dining table.

"I'm okay. Trying to keep everything running." Wayne took a pull from his beer. "Trying to keep Dad from working too hard. I wish he'd spend more time with his new girlfriend and less time at the ranch. Although I don't expect that will be a problem much longer."

Lance shifted his feet. "Why? What do you mean?"

"We'll talk about it later, when we go over the ledger."

Gwen shook her head, like she'd seen a flying saucer. Lance put his wine down on a side table. "We're not really going to do that—are we? We haven't done that for years. I can wait for Dad to mail the balance sheet and income statement." He treated the idea like an unwelcome interruption to a vacation.

"Dad wants to do it since we're all here. This morning at the ranch he said he was worried that this might be the last time we get together. He said he wanted you and Percival to be there too."

"The truth is, we've never reviewed the ledger together. When was Mary ever there? After giving her a stake, Dad never invited her. Not once." The truth of it hammered me. Lance held his hands out. "I didn't want any part of it, but Dad insisted." He dropped his hands to his sides. "I don't want to fight. We came up here so Dad could congratulate Percival." He tapped Wayne's shoulder. "I'll do whatever Dad wants, up to a point." Lance took Gwen's hand and they stepped away.

I followed them. "Have you talked to Dad yet?"

They stopped. "We said hello when we got here." Lance clipped each word. "I'm sure we'll get a chance to talk later."

Eddie stepped through the swinging door from the kitchen. "Okay everyone, dinner's ready. We could use some help carrying it out."

We filed into the kitchen, where Eddie started assigning a dish to each person.

"How are your folks doing?" Eddie handed me a bowl of sweet potatoes.

"They're okay."

Lindsey leaned in to whisper in my ear. "I think having you home helps." Mary handed Lindsey a bowl of corn and we left the kitchen.

In the dining room, Grandpa sat at the far end of the table, talking to Percival. A mountain of mashed potatoes and a gravy boat waited in front of them. Maybe, after ten years, Grandpa had figured out how to handle Percival and the shooting.

"Hi, Dad." Wayne set the sweet potatoes down. "Hey, college boy."

"Uncle Wayne." Percival stood up and grabbed his hand. "Good to see you."

I saw only a hint of the boy I remembered in the man's face in front of me. His shoulder-length hair grazed a blue dress shirt, that emphasized his olive skin. The angular features he'd inherited from Gwen gave his face a constant intensity. He looked at me with bottomless eyes. I wondered if Percival was seeing me sprawled out in the stern of the boat with my arm blown off, rather than standing before him. We stood for a moment, assessing each other, before Wayne continued the conversation.

"So, how was it?" Wayne held up his beer. "Did you learn anything?"

"I must have—they let me graduate." Percival smiled. He clinked his bottle against Wayne's. "I thought the last year would never end. It feels great to be done. If I hadn't graduated, they probably would have kicked me out for spending too much time with the shrink at the health service." He laughed and put his bottle down. "You shaved off your beard."

Wayne pointed at Lindsey. She ran her hand over his chin. "I wanted to see his handsome face again. I was starting to forget what was under there."

Percival took a drink. "How's Will?"

"He works with me at the ranch." Wayne finished his beer. "Speak of the devil."

Will set a bowl of cranberry sauce on the table, regarding Percival like someone he vaguely recognized from a past life. "It's been a long time." He sat down next to Lindsey.

"It has." Percival put his napkin in his lap.

We sat there waiting for them to say more, until Percival broke the silence. "Pelting start tomorrow?"

Grandpa rearranged himself in his chair. "Yup." His face came back to life.

Percival rotated his bottle. "Is there anything I can do?"

I'd figured they would drop in and leave like they did for Grandma's funeral. "You staying for the weekend? You sure you want to get your hands dirty?"

"Sure. Why not? I don't mind."

Will looked up sharply. "I'll put him to work, Dad."

Lance and Gwen arrived with the turkey and stuffing for our end of the table. Lance set down a plate of sliced breast meat. "What's this I overheard about work?"

"I'm going to help with pelting tomorrow." Percival said it like he was going to the movies with a friend.

Gwen puckered her face. Pulling out his chair, Lance spoke without addressing anyone. "Is that right?"

"You should come help us." Grandpa dished potatoes onto his plate. "It'll be good for you. Do some real work before you head back."

Lance glared at Percival. "I'll think about it."

Eddie led the blessing and gave thanks for continued prosperity, clearly referring to the Worland family's expanding fortune rather than the situation of the people seated in front of him. He spoke with the self-assurance of someone who had worked hard and achieved success with no personal risk. Eddie was mercifully unaware that the Almighty had started long ago to withhold his blessings from those gathered around the table.

We held hands while Eddie spoke. Mom and Dad looked tired, not from lack of sleep, but from years of sadness. When Eddie finished the blessing, our voices blended into a rising crescendo, talking through, around and over each other. On several occasions, Mary tapped her glass to keep the chatter from turning into a roar.

While the kids cleared the dinner plates and Mary brought out the pies, I ran into Lance in the hallway on my way to the bathroom. We met in front of an abstract painting that was gray and white with two red dots. We both stood there a minute looking at it. "I've never seen this painting before," I said. If Mary's signature weren't in the lower right corner, I wouldn't have recognized it as one of hers. "It's not like anything else she's done. Is it new?"

Lance looked in both directions before answering. "No, she did it when she was at St. Kate's."

"Have you seen it before?"

"Grandpa told me about it, but I hadn't seen it until today." He ran his eyes over the painting.

"What did Grandpa say about it?"

"That it bothered him."

"What do you think about it?" The white triangular shapes and red dots reminded me of the channel markers and their flashing beacons. "Have you asked her about it?"

"I don't have to. I know who it is and what it means."

"*Who* it is?" There was nothing in it that looked like a person to me.

"If you really want to know, you should ask her." He gave me a condescending pat on the back and headed down the hallway to the dining room. Standing alone in front of that painting, I wondered if anything I saw was what it appeared to be.

Back at the table, the kids passed around the pies. Wayne asked Lizzie to bring in the package she'd taken from him earlier. Grandpa, Lance and Percival compared the pumpkin pie to the apple pie, while Will and Lindsey discussed Will's new girlfriend and what she might like for Christmas. I took a slice of the apple pie when it came around.

"Here's your box, Uncle Wayne." Lizzie held it out with straight arms. "It's light." She tossed it a few inches in the air and caught it.

"Thanks Lizzie."

Percival raised his hand. "Lizzie, have you decided where you're going to school?"

She sidled around to the other side of the table and spoke as if she were sharing top secret information. "Mom wants me to go to St. Kate's." Then she lowered her voice further. "But I want to go to Bennington. What do you think?" She draped an arm around Percival's shoulder.

"Bennington, hands-down. No grades and better scenery."

"Speaking of school," Wayne said, holding out the box to me, "I got you something for graduation."

I flipped the box in the air as Lizzie had. "I don't graduate until spring. Knowing you, it's an empty box."

"What's going on at this end of the table?" Mary walked up behind me and put her hands on my shoulders. "Are you opening the mystery box now?"

"I am."

Dad held out the jackknife he always carried. I ran the blade through the seam at the top, pulled back the flaps, and reached inside.

"No way!" I held it up so Mom and Dad could see it, then showed it to Grandpa.

He took the plastic bag from my hand and held it up. "What is a Puffer Kite?"

Dad pulled up a chair and sat down between Grandpa and me. "Is this one of your gag gifts?"

Wayne put his hand on Dad's left leg. The metal and leather of the prosthesis pushed against the fabric of his pants. "Not exactly. It's an inflatable kite. I promised I'd get him one if I came to the Cities. I bought it years ago and it sat in the desk at the ranch; figured it was time to give it to him since I have no idea when I'll go to the Cities again."

Grandpa handed the bag with the kite back to me. "I've got something for each of you." He stepped over to a side table and picked up two boxes and handed one to each of us, then returned to his chair.

Percival opened his box and pulled out Grandpa's beat-up half-hull model that hung for years over the workbench at the boat shed. "Thanks, my dad told me about this." We passed the model around, and it reached Dad last. He stood up and held it by one end over the table. Percival stood up and held the opposite end. They looked at each other, holding it.

"Congratulations, Percival." Dad let go and sat down.

"Thanks, Uncle Pete." Percival returned to his seat and faced Grandpa. "I don't know what to say. Thank you." He turned to me. "I heard you made one."

"I did. It got me started in architecture." I opened my box. The leather-bound tri-fold case sat at the bottom. Inside the case were the worn but well-maintained mechanical drawing tools inset like diamonds in green velvet. I lifted out the compass and examined it.

Grandpa leaned back in his chair. "I bought those tools when I went to the University. I used them in my mechanical drawing class, then to build the house, to design the boats, and to draw plans for the mink farm." I put the compass back into the case. "Lance used them too, when he was at MIT." I handed the case to Lance.

"I remember these." He held the box like it contained the crown jewels. "You made me give these back as soon as I got home from Boston."

Lance handed the case to Mary. "I used these to make figures for art class in high school." She tumbled the pointer end-over-end through her fingers and laid it back into its slot.

Mary handed the case to Wayne. "I saw these lying around everywhere growing up—at home in Dad's office, upstairs at the fishery, in the shed where he built the boats—I never paid any attention to them. They had meant nothing more to me than the forks in the silverware drawer, until I tried to build one of the damn models myself." He handed the case to Dad.

Dad balanced it in his hands like a prayer book. He lifted out the various instruments and examined each one as if it were a clue to a great mystery, which I suppose they were to him: a set of keys to get out of Worland. He had no interest in solving that mystery. Grandpa spoke as Dad handed the case back to me.

"I used those tools to rebuild my life during the Depression. Jay, Percival, I'm proud of what you boys have done. I hope these gifts remind you over the years of who you are and where you came from."

We sat there for another hour listening to Grandpa talk about how he made design drawings for the boats and built the half-hull models, then used the models to determine the length of the keel and the planks for the hull. When he finished, he said he was tired and wanted to head home for a snooze. He asked us to come over at eight to review the ledger.

After our little group at the end of the table broke up, I went with Mary to the kitchen to help clean up. When the dishwasher started to thump and the big pots were soaking in the sink, Eddie went upstairs for a well-deserved nap, leaving Mary and me in front of three full garbage bags. Laughter from the kids in the dining room slipped under the kitchen door. Her morning energy long spent, Mary looked at the bags like they held regrets. I saw this as my chance.

"Need a hand with those?"

"Sure, let's take them out to the garage."

We walked through a narrow pantry to an open room where the coats had been hung on hooks and piled on a storage bench. I opened the door for her and followed her around the cars to the bins on the opposite side of the stalls. The cold stung after being in the house all afternoon.

"The gray-and-white painting in the hallway is unusual."

Mary lifted the top of the bin and dropped in the first bag without acknowledgment.

"It looks like the channel markers. Is that what it is?"

The car next to us was the Buick Eddie drove. He once told me he would never drive a Cadillac or one of those foreign sport sedans. It would make him uncomfortable to get out of a fancy car and face one of his employees in the parking lot of the grocery store.

Mary picked up the next bag, stopped, and set it back down. "You're the second person to see it that way." Her eyes had the same depth as Percival's.

I picked up the second bag and dropped it in the bin. "Go on."

"It is the channel markers, but it's something else too." She had her hands on her hips, like she was ready to give an art history lecture, but that was not her way. "It's the only abstract I've done, and the only one I'll ever do. I don't have another one in me. I like to paint people around town while they're lost in their work. It helps me get lost in mine, and that is where I find myself."

"Lance implied the something else is a person."

"It is—a person who never was."

She sounded to me like she was speaking in riddles. The clammy air in the garage pushed through my skin to my bones. I wanted to go back inside, get warm.

"Just tell me what it's about. What it means."

"It's about a sacrifice—of sorts."

"A sacrifice for what?"

Her eyes became moist. She made a circular gesture in the air. "For everything here. For Eddie. For the life *I* wanted."

"I don't get it."

"It's like that picture where you see the vase or the two faces. It's the same picture, but what you see depends on you, not the picture. You and your dad saw the channel markers. Percival and Lance saw the lost child."

"C'mon, there's more to it than that."

"Jay, I had an abortion during college. It was risky, and illegal. The painting guides me toward what matters, like the channel markers guide a skipper on the lake."

"And what matters? After four years of college, I have no idea."

"You must *discover* what matters."

I dropped the last bag into the bin. She put her hands on my shoulders and squeezed. "I'll see you later over at Grandpa's." We walked across the garage and back into the house.

Feeling lost, I found Mom and Dad, and we showed ourselves out.

That evening, Grandpa took the ledger out of his desk and opened it to the current year. He laid it out so we could see the red numbers at the bottom of the page. Lance turned to the previous year. Another row of red numbers. After each year, they glanced at each other.

The ink on those pages might as well have been their blood. Each year, they worked more for less, convinced that hard work always paid off, while the rest of the world took them for fools.

"I had no idea." Mary hooked her right arm around Wayne's left as Lance turned through years with red numbers. "The reports were in black and white. When the checks stopped, I assumed you put the money into equipment or something."

Lance continued until he found a row of black numbers. "I didn't realize it had been going on this long. You haven't run a profit in six years?" He rested his hand on the book. "Why didn't any of you say something?"

Wayne pulled his hand off the ledger. "What do you care? You never wanted to be a part of it in the first place. I suppose you're going to say you knew this would happen all along."

"I suspected it might." Lance left the book open at 1980, the last profitable year. "I read the papers in the Cities." He walked to the window and watched a car move past on the street.

Mary tugged on her sweater. "I asked for years to be part of this, and all of you shut me out." She dabbed at her eyes and smiled. "I don't know whether to laugh or cry."

"You can't go on like this." Lance flipped forward to the current year. "What are we going to do? The business needs cash to operate next year."

He made it sound like they could plant forty acres of cash and harvest it next summer.

"What do you suggest, Sir Lancelot?" Wayne said. "Want to buy us out? Help your poor relations?"

"Buy you out? I don't want the share I have." He sat down on the couch. "Anyway, I couldn't if I wanted to. I'm getting killed by tuition and expenses for Gwen and Aoife, and until Percival finds a job, I'm supporting him too. Ignoring that, maintenance, taxes and insurance for the ranch and the boats would still break me."

Mary sat down next to Lance. "I could buy your share—that would raise some cash." She put her hands on her knees. "You could run for a couple more years."

Grandpa closed the ledger book. "Absolutely not!"

"Why?" Mary got up off the couch.

Grandpa rose to meet her. "I'll never sell to a Worland." They stood face-to-face in the center of the room. "Cal gave me nothing for showing him how to bend wood for windows. I made him!" Dad punched the air with his finger. "He took my design. No acknowledgment, no friendship, no support. Nothing. His son got my daughter and killed her ambition. I won't do it!" His face turned red. "The only thing that son of a bitch ever gave me was a shot of scotch at your wedding."

"So that's why you never included me, isn't it? As long as there was a chance I could end up with Eddie, you were going to shut me out, and once I married him, you locked the door. Why did you give me a share in the first place?"

"Sweetheart, I wanted you to have something to fall back on, to pursue your dreams, to paint, to see the world. I thought you might see it that way too, but you never did. The day you married Eddie Worland was the saddest day of my life, until today." He took the handkerchief from his back pocket and wiped his face, then sat down in the desk chair.

Dad's leg must have been killing him. He sat next to Lance on the couch and pulled four Tylenol from a tin in his shirt pocket. He swallowed them two at a time without water. "So, what do we do now?" The pain in his voice bound the words together. Dad knew the end was coming for him in four years, when commercial fishing would no longer be allowed on the lake.

"We have to pelt them all." Dad threw his handkerchief on top of the ledger. "Eighteen thousand or we'll continue to lose money until we're flat broke."

The end was now coming for Wayne in four weeks. Fifty years and two lifetimes of work ended in a single sentence. "What about the building, the equipment, the land?"

"I'll set up an auction for the equipment next spring and sell the leftovers for scrap. After that, we can look at selling the land." Grandpa put the ledger book back in the drawer. "We've got an early start tomorrow. All of you should get home."

Mary walked to the door from where Grandpa left her standing. "I'm sleeping in tomorrow." After she'd gone, we walked to the liquor cabinet in the dining room. Grandpa pulled out the whiskey and filled shot glasses.

We drank without a toast.

Lance and I did the killing. Grandpa and Dad skinned. Will, Wayne and Percival ran the tumbler and did the stretching. There was no obvious antagonism between Dad and Percival, but Wayne made sure to keep them apart. Every time I brought a load into the shop from the yard, they looked up without saying anything. The rattle of the skinning machines and the liquid tearing of skin away from flesh was mixed with the voice of Placido Domingo.

Once when I returned to a shed after bringing a load to the building, I saw Lance holding a gray animal. He stared at its face.

"How is your dad holding up?"

"So far, he and Percival are getting along. But in the grand scheme of things, he's not doing well. He eats pills like candy. The bone spurs on his stump and the pain in his back are endless, and if he keeps at it, he's going to have a hole in his stomach."

Lance allowed the animal to squirm around in his hands while he stroked its fur.

"Will he ever take the buyout?"

"Maybe he should ask his rich older brother for help. He'll never stop fishing, not until the last day or the game warden drags him off the lake. They've got nothing left. Dad is running on fumes. To be straight with you, Mom's work at Worland's keeps them afloat, and Dad hates that. When he's done fishing, he'll probably end up at Worland's too, and that factory work will crush him."

"What's Wayne going to do?"

"He'll do anything. He's not proud, but I'm sure as hell he won't work at Worland's. He'll figure out something. He told me at Mary's he's been thinking about starting a house painting business. It's one thing the Worlands don't have their fingers in. If it's not painting houses, he could do maintenance work, drive a school bus—whatever. Maybe he and Will could do something together."

Lance put the animal over his thigh and broke its neck. The body twitched when he set it on top of the cage. He poked it to make sure it was dead.

"I guess we all have to do shit we don't like to survive."

We worked our way up and down the sheds for the rest of the afternoon. The shop was noisy when we came in with the last cart. The sound jolted me after the tranquility of killing. After we finished processing the last of the day's pelts, Dad said he and Wayne were going to the Northern Tap for a beer.

Twenty: December 1986

We drank—and killed mink. I stayed after Thanksgiving rather than return to the Cities for school. Wayne, Dad and I walked the sheds. Ministers of death. For thirty consecutive days, Thanksgiving to New Year's Eve, the blood and shit from the butchery accumulated day after day on our jackets, mittens, pants and boots. Our clothing turned into gore-covered armor in the subzero weather.

We said next to nothing to each other for all those days. Head tilts, hand flicks, and shoulder shrugs were enough. Wayne smoked roll-your-owns and Dad chewed his pills. We killed with maniacal grins, and we killed with solemn brows. We killed while doing a jig, and we killed while shaking from the cold. We killed in anger, and we killed with satisfaction. We killed with tears running down our faces, and we killed them all.

Dead is always in the present tense. Now, now, and still now. It's not like *rich*, or *smart*, or *beautiful*, which will eventually be replaced with *poor*, or *stupid*, or *ugly* as the years go by. The business is dead, a way of life is dead, and someday we'll be dead. Once that adjective is properly applied, it cannot be peeled off.

Each day started with a nightmare and a throbbing headache. The work dragged on for twelve to fifteen hours a day. Each day ended with beer and whiskey at the Northern Tap. At nearly eighty, Grandpa skinned slowly while listening to arias at a deafening volume.

The imminent Christmas holiday made no impact on our spirits. A haze of sad fatigue settled over everything. Robert came home from college in Bemidji full of energy to put up a Christmas tree. We worked on it one evening, but then it stood dark and half-decorated, without gifts underneath.

Back at the U, each night I dreamed I fell from the Worland water tower into a sea of skinned mink carcasses. I graduated with my architecture degree in the spring and returned to Worland for the summer before I started my apprenticeship that fall at a firm in the Cities.

One day in late May, Grandpa, Wayne and I drove out to the ranch together in Grandpa's new Silverado. I think he liked the idea of a nice truck more than the reality of it. All his life, he owned used trucks with bare metal floors covered by thin rubber mats. The day he got the new pickup, Dad said he drove over to our place in his bare feet with the AC blasting on a sixty-degree day. "My last truck is going to be a nice one," he said with a big smile, curling his toes into the new carpet.

We walked the fenceline while we waited for the auctioneer to arrive. The sun pushed forcefully against the cold—spring not only on the calendar, but in fact. A disturbing quiet had settled over the place. No squealing mink clawed the cages. The cooler compressor no longer kept time by starting up and shutting down. Under the awning on the back side of the building, the tractor and the feed cart sat covered in dust and bird droppings.

Grandpa climbed up on the tractor. "We had a good run." He moved the steering wheel like a kid pretending to drive. "I'm sorry we couldn't keep it going longer."

"You did the right thing, not taking Mary and Eddie's money." Wayne kicked one of the tractor's tires. "I didn't want to answer to them, and it was going to end someday, anyhow. It was as good a time to quit as any. The Russians can raise them much cheaper than we can."

"I guess that's how it's going to go from now on—win the peace and lose the economy." I helped him down from the tractor. We walked toward the gate at the west end of the yard. In the field beyond, the target rack leaned from years of being pushed by the wind. Pieces of broken bottles lay strewn on the ground.

"I never beat you." Wayne rasped his boot over the shards. Somewhere underfoot were the bottles Will, Percival and I shot, buried by the ones Lance, Pete, Grandpa, and Wayne hit, and still more broken by the other boys when they learned to shoot.

"You could beat me now." Grandpa stood on a section of the bare patch where the snow had melted. "I could barely see the damn targets. You were always too wild to be a great shot."

"Ah, the undefeated Sir Lancelot," Wayne said.

Grandpa adjusted his coat. "We better head back. The auction guys are probably waiting."

The auctioneer had parked his flatbed truck parallel to the building. He set up a podium in the middle of the truck bed and a desk at the end to collect payments. I drove the tractor out from behind the building and parked it next to the auctioneer's truck. Wayne and the auctioneer brought things from inside to sell in lots. Pneumatic drill and bits, impact wrench and sockets, the portable compressor. Welder, torches, masks, brazing rods and clamps. Stools, work benches and racks. The mower for the tractor. A trailer-mounted feed auger.

From inside the shop, we heard the auctioneer's rat-a-tat call. The disconnected skinning machines did not hum. No static came from the old radio. When the welding equipment sold for twenty dollars, Grandpa grimaced and shook his head. Alice went on the block last. The bidding dragged on, going up in ridiculously small increments: fifty cents, a dollar twenty-five, seventy-five cents. She finally sold for ninety dollars—cheap—to a tractor collector from the Cities.

After everyone hauled their purchases away and the auctioneer's truck rumbled back toward town, odd tools and equipment lay spread out in front of the ranch building like abandoned children, waiting for parents who would never return.

The night after the auction, Wayne called Dad to ask him to meet at the Northern Tap. Mom answered and said she would see to it Dad showed up, even if she had to put him in his truck herself. I spent the summer wondering what they might have said to each other, until I ran into Wayne outside the post office one late-August afternoon.

"You look like you're on your way out of town," Wayne said.

"I am. I start my apprenticeship on Monday."

"Who are you going to work for?"

I told him.

"Never heard of them." He stood there for a moment. "I don't have much useful advice to give, but I can tell you this—work for yourself. Your boss will be an asshole, but he'll pay you better than anyone else."

"Do you remember that night after the auction, when you called my dad, and you met him at the Northern Tap?"

"I do. I'll never forget it."

"What happened? He came home haunted, like he'd seen a ghost."

Wayne tilted his head up at the water tower. The sun glinted off the polished steel. The crossed hockey sticks above the town's name appeared in his eyes.

He started by saying they hadn't seen each other beyond chance crossings in the grocery store or at mass. On those rare occasions, once they'd exhausted talking about how Grandpa was doing, they had nothing more to say. They used to talk constantly, they couldn't help it, spending nearly every day working together, but the ritual conversations didn't work anymore. They moved like planets orbiting a dying star, eclipsing each other, waiting for the black hole left behind to obliterate them.

Dad had declined to come to the auction, saying he needed to mend nets, which Wayne said was true, but also an excuse. He had thought a gesture to Dad—his invitation to the Tap—might restore their camaraderie, which he missed.

Wayne waited for Dad outside in the pool of light under the Hamm's sign. As he shifted his feet, the sense of what he wanted to say vaporized. Dad's truck emerged from the darkness and a stretched reflection of the sign slid up the windshield. He stepped out of the truck. Wayne was happy to see him, noticing in his face a fading resemblance to Grandma. As he pulled open the door to the Tap, the warm air from inside, with its scent of damp wool, peanuts and tobacco, wafted over them.

They sat on two stools at the corner of the bar. On a television mounted to the ceiling, red- and blue-clad hockey players swirled around fluorescent ice. Wayne looked up at the screen, while Dad spun a coaster. Shorty Amundsen, the bar tender, sauntered over.

"What'll it be?"

Wayne held up his wallet. "Two Hamm's and two shots of Jameson."

Shorty looked at Dad, who nodded.

Wayne said he saw his nineteen-year-old self on the television. A scholarship hockey player who wanted to avoid this place and this day, but the goals and the degree hadn't come. The Air Force, Lindsey and the kids, they did come.

Shorty returned with the drinks. He put them on the bar, then stared at the screen.

"We're fine," Wayne said. What they said to each other was nobody's damn business. Shorty walked away.

A player in a red jersey looped around the net, then backhanded the puck into the lower right corner. A few lazy cheers went up from the tables.

"*Sláinte*." They drank the shots.

Dad slammed his glass on the bar. "Just like you. Backhand always was your style."

Wayne turned away from the game. The warmth in his chest brought a receding memory of youthful exuberance, the sensation itself long out of reach.

"At least I had a style, and some ambition beyond—"

"Why did you and your ambition bother to come back? Dad was right when he said you couldn't finish anything." Meanness did not come naturally to Dad as it did to Wayne. The remark felt pathetic rather than insulting, a failed attempt to make him feel as bad as Dad did. Dad didn't know Wayne already felt as bad or worse, and that he didn't need to do anything to find a companion in sorrow. Still, Wayne wasn't going to allow his gloom to take his sense of humor, so he made a gesture to Dad at his own expense.

"I had no choice. And by the way, I did finish something—I finished off the mink ranch." He clinked his glass against Dad's.

Dad chuckled. "Goddamnit, I hate how you can make me laugh." He took a swig of beer. "You finished it off all right."

An official dropped the puck and play resumed. Wayne followed the red skaters swirling around the blue skaters.

"Why did Dad ask me to wash the boat? Why not Lance?"

"I wanted you to see it."

"Well, I saw it."

Dad raised his mug from the bar as if he were about to give a toast, hesitated, then drank the contents. He studied Wayne's eyes, perhaps searching for an indication that what he'd seen had the desired effect.

"At least the old man spared you." Wayne lifted his glass and finished his beer in a series of gulps.

Dad called down to Shorty for two more, then asked Wayne about the auction. As Wayne was telling him about it, Dad looked up at the TV, stood up and said he had to go. He couldn't listen to it anymore.

"What was on the TV?" I asked.

Wayne told me. On the television, gloves littered the ice. Two players were against the boards, each trying to pull the other closer with one hand, while punching with the other.

Twenty-one: October 1990

It was a beautiful day to go fishing. The wind was light. Snowflakes fluttered down in the near-freezing air. When Dad and I arrived at the fishery, several men were waiting outside. One man followed us in to where the oilers hung underneath the stairs.

"Do you have any walleye for sale?"

"Nope." Dad didn't look at him as he reached for his gear.

"Will you have any after you come in?"

"Nope." He pulled on his boots. "You had to order two weeks ago."

"Any northerns?"

"I may have some to spare. Come back in about four hours."

"Any saugers or perch, or anything?"

"I can get you all the tullibees and suckers you want and sell them to you real cheap. No mink ranches around anymore to take them."

"You'd have to pay me to take those. Know where I can get walleyes?"

"I'm the last commercial fisherman on Lake of the Woods and the last walleye fisherman in the United States."

"What happened to all the fishermen that used to be around here?"

"You need to talk to the friendly politicians in St. Paul. If you want to buy Lake of the Woods fish, you need to go to Canada."

He buttoned up his oiler jacket. This day had been eight years coming. What he did, and what I thought I would do for my entire life would be done for the last time on this day. If Dad wasn't a fisherman, he was lost. Jesus called St. Peter away from his nets to fish for men. No one called Dad away from his to do anything.

We walked out onto the dock and loaded fish boxes into the boat. We weren't in a hurry. We had two nets to lift and didn't expect much out of them. The old Ford diesel engine started on the first try despite the cold weather. The day seemed abnormal because it was. If it hadn't been the last day of the last commercial fishing season on Lake of the Woods, I would have said it was almost pleasant.

Roger sat on the stack of fish boxes as we headed out on the river. A flock of ducks rose from the reeds on the north side and passed over us, heading south toward the channel markers. No other boats were docked on the river or plowing through the waves on the open lake. All the sportos packed it in Labor Day weekend, back to the Cities for school, office jobs and politics.

In the distance, Elm Point revealed itself. It was the best walleye and northern spot on the lake. Dad owned six pound net licenses, but he'd pulled four nets at the beginning of October and left two in the water for the last day. I lined the boat up for the approach to the first net. Roger stood ready with the bow line, and Dad handled the stern.

We started to lift the net. Roger peeked at the rocky shoreline after every pull.

"How does it feel?" Dad said.

Roger put his hands on the gunwale. "Like I'm home. No matter how far away I go or what I do, I can't leave this place behind. But I've been pushing too much goddamn paper. I can't do this kind of work anymore. How did you manage thirty years without killing yourself?"

"Counselor, what makes you think I haven't?"

Roger held a tangle of black net chest high. His face was clean shaven, and he wore a canvas cap over his thinning hair. "You saved me. I would have been a terrible soldier."

We picked gilled walleyes out of the net and tossed them back into the water. They swam away with a few scales missing. Four dollars from our pockets, destined for some sporto's hook. It had been a good walleye and northern season, better than if Dad had taken the buyout. Roger tossed a nice walleye into an empty fish box.

"Save that one for me. You want to use the power dipper to finish?"

It was mounted on a steel frame above the pilothouse, moving back and forth with the swells. If I looked close enough, I probably could have found blood on the cable.

"No. Let's do it the old-fashioned way and use the hand dipper. There isn't much here."

We filled twenty-four boxes with northerns and walleyes. Rather than reset the pounds, we removed them from the pilings and heaped them in the bow. We headed back to Worland. At the fishery, more people were waiting than when we left. The guy who wanted the northerns was waiting too. He watched us haul the fish boxes and heaped nets up from the deck like he was watching a horse-drawn plow demonstration. Roger washed down the deck while the customers who ordered their walleye two weeks ago collected their fish. After all the other customers were gone, most of whom left empty-handed, Dad approached the man who waited.

"You want 'em dressed or raw?"

"I prefer them naked."

He put three fish on the scale. The man handed him a twenty-dollar bill. The last walleye and the last two northerns were sold. Dad wrapped them carefully in waxed paper and sealed the package with masking tape. The man walked out the loading door to his car. There were no more fish for sale.

Roger came into the dark, open room carrying the life ring and four life jackets. He dropped them on the floor.

"What do you want to do with the compass, the radio and the rifle?"

"Take out the radio and the compass and leave the rifle," Dad said.

The sound of the lake sloshing underneath the planking bounced around the room. When we finished, we took off our oilers and hung them on the hooks below the stairs. Roger kicked off his boots and put on his shoes.

"Are you sure you want to go through with it? You can stop now."

"I'm sure," Dad said.

"What about your dad and Wayne?"

"We're all sure."

The next morning, as the first rays of sun flared up from the horizon, Wayne drove us out to the ranch in his painting truck. I didn't like to go out there since we shut down the operation. The quiet of the vacant sheds heightened my emptiness. Four years after we pelted the last mink, I could still hear claws clicking on cage wire and the squealing of newborn kits. Wayne stopped in front of the building. A conspicuous stillness pervaded the place.

"Creepy, ain't it?"

Roger took in the scenery. "It is. This is nice property. It's a shame to see it go."

"Wayne, where's the farm truck and boat trailer? We need to get this done so we're not holding up the Worland people on Lake Street."

It's not that Dad gave a damn about holding up the Worland people; he said he didn't want to turn taking the boat out into a parade of sorrows. No one needed to see it.

Wayne led us out to the junk yard where he'd parked the farm truck, with the trailer already hitched, on the access road. Wayne pulled open the door.

"Pete, you wanna drive?"

"No thanks. It would feel like I was driving a hearse with my own coffin."

Wayne got behind the wheel. Roger and I sat in the middle.

"Is Arthur going to meet us there?"

Dad got in and closed the door. "No, he'll meet us back here. Wayne, did you fill the gas cans?"

"Yup. They're in the back."

At the fishery, Wayne backed the trailer up to the slip while Roger and I unmoored the boat. Dad piloted the boat away from the dock and lined it up with the trailer. He took the rifle off its rack in the pilothouse.

"Roger, I thought you might want this." Dad handed it to him. "The only time it got taken out with the intent to use it was when you went over the side."

Roger held it with open hands, as if it burned his palms. "Pete, I don't know what to say."

Wayne walked to the edge of the slip. "What the hell are you guys yakking about, we need to get going. I have a painting job to get to. Come on."

He threw the winch cable over the bow, and Dad secured it to the head cleat. We climbed over the gunwale into the shallow water and splashed our way onto the slip. Wayne engaged the winch and pulled the boat onto the trailer.

At the ranch, we towed the boat into the northwest corner of the junk yard. Grandpa sat in the field on one of the old office chairs from the workshop. He got up and walked over as Dad and Wayne unhitched the trailer.

"Have any trouble getting her out?" He sounded like he expected her to have put up a fight, like a terrified prisoner on the way to the gallows.

"Nope. She came out as smooth as the day she went in."

Dad stepped back from the trailer hitch. Wayne handed the gas cans to me from the truck bed, then drove the truck over to the collapsed target rack and parked it. Dad climbed aboard. Grandpa handed him a cable cutter and a ratchet with a quarter-inch socket. Roger wandered around the field, looking at the rusted machinery strewn about. Dad cut the steering cable and removed the bolts holding the helm, then handed the helm to Grandpa with the cutter and the ratchet. He asked me to hand up a gas can.

When he came back from the truck, Wayne climbed on board. I handed him the other gas can. They splashed fuel over the deck, dribbled it on the forward gunwale, and climbed back down. Roger opened his hand to show us two arrowheads he'd found: one black and one red.

Wayne held up his stainless-steel lighter.

"Pete? Dad?"

Grandpa handed the helm to me and grabbed the lighter.

"I built it. I'll burn it."

He walked to the bow, flicked open the top of the lighter, and struck the wheel. The flame rose and swayed in the low morning breeze. He paused to survey the yard, then tilted his wrist forward. Flames engulfed the boat.

The heat forced us to take a few steps back. We stood surrounded by the rotting fruit of our labor. Roger took my hand and pressed the arrowheads into my palm.

I saw no beginning and no end, a parade of years stretching from the primordial past to a vanishing point where everything disintegrates.

Twenty-two: March 2009

Mom's call came in the middle of a home design review with a health insurance executive, one of many of my high-profile clients I had designed homes for, including business leaders, professional athletes and prominent artists. I'd also designed a contemporary, prairie-style office building that housed the architecture and engineering practice Percival and I owned. Percival managed the engineering and construction.

Nineteen years before, at the reception following Grandpa's funeral, Percival and I had found ourselves sitting alone together at a table. Grandpa had died from a heart attack, sitting on a park bench under the St. Louis Arch. He'd gone on a bus tour five months after setting fire to the boat and hadn't made it back home. Even though both Percival and I lived in the Cities, we hadn't seen each other in five years, since the Thanksgiving when Grandpa decided to close the mink farm. We sat there complaining to each other about our corporate jobs: mine at a commercial architecture firm designing glass-box office buildings, and his at a civil engineering firm managing the design and construction of electric substations.

Wayne and Lindsey came upon us mid-complaint. The only remainders of the vibrant people I knew as a kid were their eyes and their smiles.

"Hey, city slickers. I wasn't sure if you were going to try and slip away without saying hello." He took my hand like he was going to put it over his thigh and break it. The tattoo on his neck had faded to illegibility. If there had been a tattoo artist at the reception, I'd have gotten one just like it. "What are you two talking about?"

"Trying to figure out what to do with ourselves," I said.

"We're good at jobs we don't like and don't know what to do next," Percival added. "How about you?"

"I'm at home driving the old lady nuts, except when I go to the casino." They sat down, and Wayne drank from a cup of black coffee. "And don't worry too much about figuring out what to do. Life has a way of doing that for you." He gave Lindsey a long kiss.

A big smoke-stained smile spread across her face. "You better watch yourself. I could still follow those instructions on your neck."

Their laughter subsided. Wayne turned to Percival. "So, what's your dad been up to, other than spending your inheritance on tropical cruises. He doesn't seem to want to talk much."

"He doesn't like coming to Worland. He reads, works on his cars. He's taking a German class." Percival poured himself a short coffee. "I won't be getting an inheritance. They're going to be the first to take it with them." At first, I thought this was clever, but then its pettiness settled on me. I had already received my inheritance—I was sitting in the middle of it.

"Jay, listen to me for a change—you two could work together." Wayne and Lindsey stood up. "I've told you before, work for yourself, be your own boss…think about it." As they walked away they held each other up, as if they were taking shelter on a windy street.

"What do you think?" I asked.

"I don't need to think about it. He's right, and I owe you. We should do it."

"Grandpa told me once that he didn't want to hear any complaints from me, and now here I am ten years later complaining at his funeral." I said it without thinking, and it rattled me.

Percival extended his hands, palms up. "So? Are you going to keep complaining, or do what Grandpa told you to do?"

"I don't know anything about starting a business."

"Neither do I, but I do know that if Wayne can start a successful house painting business, we can start an architecture and engineering practice."

I held out my left hand for Percival to shake. He refused.

"Nope," he said. "We're doing this the right way, the traditional way. Time to put the past behind us."

He grabbed my hand clamp. We shook on it.

"Brennan and Brennan," I said. "And my name is first on the sign."

I excused myself from the design review and went to my office. Mom told me Dad was not well, and I needed to come to Worland immediately.

It was dark when I arrived. I went directly to the rest home. Inside, the low fluorescent light imparted a washed-out appearance to everything, like when the lights come on in a bar after last call. A small crucifix hung on the wall above the bed, a reminder of my long-abandoned faith. On the bedside table, an electronic photo frame cycled through pictures of Dad to the faint sound of *Willie and the Poor Boys*.

I didn't recognize him. Dad's puffy cheeks and taut lips distorted his face. His hair had faded from brown to a sickly tan, and long strands dangled over his ears. If I hadn't seen his chest rise and fall, his waxy skin would have convinced me he'd died.

I watched images of the man I knew—with Mom, on the lake holding nets, at Thanksgiving—slide onto the screen, then disappear in an explosion of electronic confetti. After I watched a full cycle of the pictures, I sat next to the bed. The oxygen hissed inside the mask over Dad's nose and mouth.

Mom came into the room and laid her right hand on my forearm. I tried to find the woman next to me in the scrolling pictures, but she was gone. Mom's eyes were clear and moist. As I studied her, with pictures and memories washing through my mind, I understood how time had transformed her face from the one fixed in my mind to the one in front of me. The silence went on long enough to verge on awkwardness. We hadn't seen each other in nineteen years, not since Grandpa's funeral. Percival and I had agreed that our lives and work would only go one direction from that point on—forward.

"Hi Mom."

"He's been asking for you."

I'm certain her years as a nurse gave her the ability to summon a gentle bedside manner under those awful circumstances. It was clear by the way she carried herself that this was how she and Dad survived what life had laid upon them.

"I'm struggling, but it's not important." I realized I'd gone to Worland to say in person what I hadn't been able to say all those years ago. I knew it wouldn't make any difference and still had to be said. There are things which can never be made right, where the only way to live with them is to embrace the pain. "I'm sorry for what happened, for shutting him out, for shutting you out."

"You need to tell him, not me."

"I'm awake. I'm not dead, even though I may look like it," Dad said.

"I didn't mean to humiliate you, to embarrass you," I said. "I only wanted to know the truth, to know you suffered and were scared enough to wet your pants, like I was. I wanted to know you understood what I'd been through. Instead, you lied to me. After that, I decided I had to leave and find my own way."

He turned his head toward the opposite wall. Mom dabbed his face with a cloth. He looked back at me. "I'm proud of what you've done, what you've achieved. At least between the two of us there's one man in full." His head sank into the pillow with fatigue.

"You'd better go," Mom said. "He's tired. Come back tomorrow when you've both had some rest. He couldn't keep still after I told him you were on your way."

At the funeral reception, in the meeting room of the new Catholic church, I started and finished, with Aunt Mary and Eddie. Lance and Gwen were on a cruise ship off the coast of Brazil, and Wayne had finally succumbed to cirrhosis the previous year. They sat with ease under the vaulted ceiling amid a swirl of grandchildren pulling on their sleeves.

"It's a beautiful building. You and Percival did a great job. Pete was proud as hell of you," Eddie said.

The place was erected to honor someone I didn't believe existed. Percival and I had sent a manager to oversee the construction rather than go ourselves.

Eddie leaned back in his chair to shake my hand. "How are you doing?"

"The financial crisis turned my life upside down. How are you?"

"Worried. Business is bad. We've had to put everyone on thirty-two-hour weeks to avoid layoffs." He scanned the room as if surveying his subjects. His jauntiness annoyed me. As if by following a few simple steps, anyone could have a comfortable and secure existence.

"I haven't the foggiest idea what I'm going to do. Percival and I will figure it out when we get back to the Cities."

Aunt Mary hugged me. "I know how that feels." She held me out at arm's length, her eyes like beacons. "Listen to your old auntie—you've done everything you set out to do. You may not believe it, but this is an opportunity. Take a break, step back." Mary turned me by the shoulders, her face close to mine. "Get the life you want, not the one everyone told you to have." She patted me on the back.

After I reintroduced myself to various cousins, I left the church and drove around town. As I grew up and spent time there, Worland never changed. I suppose that's why I didn't expect to see any major changes now either, twenty years after Dad sold the last fish.

I drove south of town to the mink ranch road. I wanted to see the sheds and the tractor and the building, the target rack, the junk cars and the tall grass. But it was gone. Instead, there was a neatly painted sign for *Ranch Estates*. It looked like a million other suburban cul-de-sacs, named for what had been destroyed and replaced. The houses had grand entries and large appendages with tall windows overlooking the frozen river. At the end of the road was a paved circle where the ranch building once stood. The place I had learned to fire a shotgun was now a snow-covered hill with a neglected wooden play structure on top.

The ground at the cemetery was frozen. A northwesterly with a hint of spring blew unimpeded over the gravestones. I had to kick away the crusty snow to find the markers. Grandpa and Grandma were under a matching red monolith. All that work to help me get away, and I was what they had to show for it. It only confirmed that my not having children had been the right decision.

I continued back to town and followed Lake Street, past Mary's house, to the end of the road where the Number Two once stood. It, too, was only a patch of circular pavement. The reeds in the marsh were brown and stiff. The lake spread out before me like a white desert under a grand, pale dome.

I looked for the duck blind stake. A city worker must have pulled it when they landscaped the shoreline. Percival had pulled the trigger, yet at the same time, there was a shared responsibility. The people of Worland allowed young boys to hunt unsupervised, engaged in grinding, relentless work, drank to excess when they finished, and meted out disproportionate punishment. There comes a time when nature demands restitution for making a living from death. Sitting there and looking at the point where Worland's culture once converged, I knew I'd spend the rest of my life making payments for what happened there.

My last stop was the fishery. It had been replaced with a brown, metal sided pole barn that housed the Five Tribes Casino. There were four cars parked out front where Dad and Grandpa used to park their trucks. I went inside and navigated my way around the blackjack tables, roulette wheels and slot machines to the windows on the opposite side of the room. Across the river stood the collapsed and rotting remains of the channel markers. The red beacons flashed in my mind. A young Native American waitress startled me when she asked if I wanted a drink. I asked for a shot of Jameson—neat.

I sat down at a slot machine, its beeps and bells enticing me to play. The woman returned with my whiskey. I bid *sláinte* to my relatives and their departed way of life. Before my eyes, Worland slipped away, and with it the buildings and the channel markers and the pound nets, revealing a winter's day generations ago when a party of Ojibwe walked along the lakeshore and saw strange-looking people covered in furs part the reeds and the tamaracks. The native people forced to wonder, for one last precipice of a moment, if the strangers were friendly or honest or good.

And now, after one hundred years, everything we'd both worked for was gone.

So I took a quarter out of my pocket—and dropped it into the machine.

Acknowledgments

Thanks to Peter Geye and my cohort in The Novel Writing Project at The Loft Literary Center for their immense patience and support in the development of this novel.

I'm grateful for the encouragement and manuscript feedback from my colleagues in the Stone Arch Workshop: Kurt Johnson, Rosanna Staffa, Debra Blake, Paula Granquist, Lisa Larson, Rachel MacDonald, and Sue Telander.

Many thanks to Michele Rubin at Cornerstones Literary Consultancy—I couldn't have done it without you.

Profound gratitude to copy editor Brittany Kallman Arneson for saving me from drowning in punctuation.

To Ian Graham Leask and Gary Lindberg at Calumet Editions, thanks for your sound advice on the manuscript and faith in me.

To Edie Hill, language is not up to the task of expressing my gratitude. You've shown what it means to be an artist through devotion to family, friends, craft, and the artistic community. You are an inspiration and artist nonpareil.

Heartfelt thanks to Deborah Kreuze for spending hours on the phone to help me get the manuscript over the finish line.

I'm forever indebted to Pilar Gerasimo for showing me the way of *The Healthy Deviant*. Your relentless pursuit of better ways to live is a profound inspiration. You enabled my recovery from decades in the Unhealthy Default Reality and showed me how to maintain body-mind health through the challenges of finishing this novel.

Thanks to Carol Schneider for sticking with me through a lifetime of ups and downs and providing a writer's retreat when I needed one.

Cheri Louck deserves a medal for reading the manuscript aloud numerous times and her patience with my interruptions.

To the Johnston and Marvin clans of Warroad, Minnesota. You are the heart and soul. Thanks to Alvin and Arthur Johnston for their fine memoir, *A Time to Fish and a Time to Dry Nets*, which provided invaluable background.

The staff of the Warroad Heritage Center displayed amazing patience with my constant requests for photographs and specific editions of the *Warroad Pioneer*.

To Dan Blank for his guidance on marketing, media, and publicity.

Thanks to Jon Lane and the cyclists of Lakeside Velo for all the great rides and companionship. Seeing you every week got me through some dark and difficult times.

With gratitude and awe for my phenomenally intelligent and accomplished siblings, Louis, Jennifer, and Mark.

To my mother Rita, for a lifelong devotion to education and literacy.

To my father Jack, I'm sorry I didn't finish in time.

About the Author

Christopher Johnston has published short fiction, travel writing, performed as a storyteller on *The Moth Mainstage*, and writes *Changing Gears* on Substack. He worked for 35 years as an engineer and management consultant, which took him to rural communities with struggling businesses throughout North America and Europe. He was born and raised in Minnesota, where he grew up around the family fishing and mink ranching businesses.